Last Chances
Jeanne Bannon

Copyright © 2018 by Jeanne Bannon

~ DEDICATION ~

For Veronica, the sweetest girl I know.

Last Chances

Copyright Warning

Copyright © 2018 by Jeanne Bannon

All rights reserved. No part of this publication may be reproduced, distributed, or transmitted in any form or by any means, including photocopying, recording, or other electronic or mechanical methods, without the prior written permission of the publisher, except in the case of brief quotations embodied in critical reviews and certain other non-commercial uses permitted by copyright law.

This book is a work of fiction. The names, characters, places, and incidents are fictitious or have been used fictitiously, and are not to be construed as real in any way. Any resemblance to persons, living or dead, actual events, locales, or organizations is entirely coincidental.

All Rights Reserved. No part of this book may be used or reproduced in any manner whatsoever without written permission, except in the case of brief quotations embodied in critical articles and reviews.

~ One ~

Monday, November 13th

Pressley entered the Paws and Claws Animal Shelter to the yelps and barks of the animals sheltered there. It was her new workplace, hopefully. The job interview had been over the phone, kind of unconventional, but the woman on the other end seemed happy enough with her responses, or, Pressley considered, maybe it was desperation she'd heard in her voice.

She looked around the small office situated at the front of the building. A thin dusting of animal hair covered every surface, and on the window ledge, three half-dead house plants, still in the green plastic containers they'd been bought in, sat in a sad row in order of height — a tall, but withering cactus was first in line; followed by an over-watered African violet with its brown, mushy-looking leaves; and finally, an unrecognizable lump of something green enough to look as if it was still alive.

An old battered desk was pushed against the far wall, while another equally well-used desk sat below a cutout in the drywall at the entranceway to the office. Pressley was thankful she had no allergies to animals or dust — this place would be hell for anyone with that affliction, and she wanted nothing more than to work with animals: to help find them homes and to take care of them.

She was peeking through the cutout looking for Janet, her new boss, when the sound of a door slamming caught her attention. She turned in time to spot a woman walking toward her from the end of a long hallway.

"Hi! Sorry, hon. I was in back with the barkers and kitty cats." The woman had dark blonde hair that looked as if it had been molded into a helmet. She was short and plump — a sharp contrast to Pressley's tall, slender frame. She smiled at Pressley as she made her way to the other side of the partition and took her place at the desk. "What can I do for you? You here to pick out a furry friend?"

"Uh, no. I'm Pressley James. We spoke on the phone last Friday? You said to come in today." Pressley smiled uncomfortably and tried to replay the conversation in her mind. Had the woman actually said, "you got the job," or was Pressley making a stupid assumption? She felt her face flush and soon sweat beaded on her forehead. Summer was long gone, but it suddenly felt like high noon on a July day.

"Yes! I'm so sorry, hon. I totally forgot. It's been too darn busy around here lately with Jess leaving so unexpectedly and all.

We're short-staffed, but then again—" she shrugged "—I hate to say it, but it's a revolving door around here sometimes. We get someone in because they simply *love* animals, but when they realize it's not just about playing with puppies and kittens all day, they leave pretty quick." She narrowed her eyes as if assessing Pressley. "You're clear about that, right? It's office work first and helping with the animals second — when you've got extra time. And, by helping, I mean cleaning up poop and pee and whatever else." She laughed. "It also means brushing and feeding and yes, playing, but only after the grunge work is done."

Pressley nodded. "Yes, ma'am, I understand. I'm ready to work."

"Don't you ma'am me! Call me Janet. I may be older than you, but I ain't your grandma. Now, come on over to the business side of this sorry excuse of a window and set yourself down over there." Janet pointed to the other side of the room where the sad-looking desk sat.

Pressley walked over, opened the bottom drawer and was about to plop her purse in, but it was filled with old files. She hung her bag on the back of her chair instead, making sure it was zipped up and smoothing the leather, so it wouldn't lose its shape. The layer of dust and fur on the desk top was making her nervous. Would it be rude if she went in search of paper towel or cleaning supplies? Or maybe she could nonchalantly blow the crud away when Janet wasn't looking?

Her new boss swiveled in her chair to face Pressley. "So, you here for the love of animals? 'Cause I know it can't be for the money with what we're paying you."

"Not for the money, no. I just need a job. It's important to have a purpose." Pressley sat primly, hands folded in her lap, the toes of her sensible shoes tapping the linoleum.

"You're in the right place, then." Janet winked. "You kids are great with social media and the Internet and all that, so whenever you're ready, power up that old clunker of a computer and get started on boosting our web presence and such. At least the monitor's fairly new. Gotta be thankful for small favors." Janet turned halfway in her chair, then swiveled back around. "Oh, and don't mind the mess. You'll get used to it soon enough."

Pressley wasn't sure she'd ever get used to the tickle of animal fur in her nose, allergic or not, it was annoying, and it hit fast, like a swarm of black flies. She waved a hand to clear the air, but it made things worse. Three ferocious sneezes escaped her. Each was met with a hearty, "God bless you" from Janet and then, "You'll get used to that, too. The fur's flying a bit more because there's two of us in here stirring it up. Got some Windex in the bottom of that cabinet and some paper towel. You can clean up later, if ya like." She indicated a lopsided wooden tower with two shelves and a cupboard at the bottom.

Pressley did like that notion, but first she'd try to get some work done — nothing like being dropped right into the mix, she thought, but then again, no one had to tell Pressley how to navigate social media. She was a Millennial; it was in her blood. Though she did think it was funny Janet had called her a *kid*. At twenty-seven, she hardly felt like a kid — here she was pushing thirty, no husband, no children, and still trying to find purpose in life.

She opened the door on the side of her desk and was shocked to see an ancient computer tower, circa 1998, complete with two floppy disk drives. It took a second to find the power button and even longer before the monitor flickered to life. Social media and marketing were right up her alley, but she needed her Mac Book Pro. There was no way she could work with this dinosaur.

Janet was shuffling through a stack of papers on her desk — another antiquated way to do business, Pressley thought — but no sooner had she navigated to the Paws and Claws' website, then Janet started talking again.

"What the heck, let's go out back now. I bet you're dying to see all the cuties we got staying with us. You can get back to work in a bit." Janet was on her feet and disappeared around the corner before Pressley could respond. She wondered where she should stash her purse. What if someone came in while they were in the back? She considered taking it with her but decided instead to stick it under her desk and push the chair in as far as it would go. Pressley jogged out of the office and down the hallway to catch up with a surprisingly speedy Janet.

"Now, before we go through this door, there are two things you need to know," Janet said, her expression sober.

Pressley thought a laugh or smile would follow. Janet seemed to be a bit of a fun-loving kidder, but the woman's expression remained stony.

"Okay, what are they?" Pressley asked.

Janet cleared her throat. "We have a fellow who works here, not a volunteer but a full-timer. He's a bit of a loner. Don't pay no mind if he doesn't give you the time of day. You're a pretty young thing and probably used to male attention." She lowered her voice as if she was about to tell a secret. "You don't mind me saying that a little makeup would make you a real stunner, do ya? And maybe let that hair down?" She slapped a hand over her mouth and looked contrite. "Shoot. Look at me being a dumb ass. I just met ya, and here I am giving beauty advice." She waved a dismissive hand. "I got a big ole mouth and usually my foot's stuck in it. Anyway, his name's Hayden and well, he's quite the looker. I've worked here long enough to know his story, but when anyone tries to break down his walls, he shuts 'em down like a twenty-car pileup on the freeway. Best to keep your distance. We need him since he's the only full-time fella. Big muscles and all that, you know — good for helping with the heavy lifting." She finally smiled, but it quickly faded. "So, the second thing to be mindful of is Jasper—"

"Jasper?" Pressley cut in. Didn't Janet just say there was only one male employee?

"Jasper's a lost cause, so don't go feeling all bad for him. We tried our best, honey. I mean, we really tried. We don't like to see any animals put down but sadly, there's no hope for him. He's a mean son of a gun and we just can't seem to find him a forever home." Janet pulled open the door. "Got it?"

Pressley nodded. Jasper was a dog whose days were numbered. Despite the warning, her heart sank at the prospect of his demise.

The back room was large, with kennels lining both sides. It was long too. From where she stood, Pressley couldn't see where it ended. It looked as if there was a corner at the wall farthest from her. She scanned the room for both Hayden and Jasper, but all she saw were what looked like tiny jail cells, occupied by barking, yelping, and meowing inhabitants. And, to her surprise, it looked a bit cleaner in the back than in the office.

Janet continued, "We pride ourselves on being a no-kill shelter. I mean, look around. Soooo many animals without owners and we do our darndest to find someone to love them. Some are long-term residents, like ole Romeo here." Janet made her way to a lump of a beagle who was curled up in an old bed. When he spotted Janet, he hobbled over, tail wagging. "Got a luxating patella. Ain't he just the sweetest boy you've ever seen?" Janet bent down and stuck a hand through the bars of the cage to scratch Romeo behind the ears.

Romeo, for his part, looked as if he was loving every moment.

"Luxating what?" Pressley asked.

"It's a knee thing. It pops out of joint every now and then. He's okay though. Too old for surgery, so he gets by on his three good legs. Romeo, the vet figures, is about fifteen so he's a lifer. Been here three years now, and I suppose he's gonna stay until the end of his days."

"Then why can't you do the same for Jasper?" Pressley couldn't help but ask the obvious.

Janet fixed her with a look of concern. "Come on over and meet that rascal. You'll see for yourself why we can't keep him."

Jasper was isolated in a corner by the back door. He had a large cage, a comfy-looking doggie bed, a bowl for food, another for water and a chew toy. Janet made her approach tentatively even though the dog was safely behind bars.

At first, all Pressley saw was the cage. Jasper, she figured, must be in the farthest corner. As she made her way closer, a few steps behind Janet, she heard a low growl, and then the snapping of teeth. Janet jumped back and when she did, Pressley laid her eyes on the most beautiful creature she'd ever seen. Her instinct was not to run or even freeze on the spot, but to move toward the dog, hand outstretched. Before Janet could stop her, she was at the cage. Jasper's growls turned to curious sniffs as he nosed Pressley's hand.

"What are you doin'?" Janet took hold of Pressley's arm and tried to pull her away.

"Shhh," Pressley said, more to the dog than to Janet. Janet muttered something under her breath about being careful, but let go her grip and watched.

Pressley moved slowly down to a crouch. Jasper kept a watchful eye on her every move, but he wasn't skittish. He held his ground. Satisfied with his preliminary investigation of Pressley's hand, she inched her hand farther into the cage, so she could pet him. He was a big boy, a German shepherd/mastiff mix if she were to guess. His fur was short and dark brown, his snout long and his nose, wet and black. But it was his eyes that Pressley loved the most. They were chocolate brown and inquisitive. How could Janet not see the intelligence behind them?

"Hey there," Pressley whispered, and the dog tucked his snout under her hand, urging her to keep petting him. "Are you a good boy?" She stroked the dog's neck. Jasper pressed up against the cage with his whole body, and Pressley had to stop herself from putting her face close. She wanted to kiss him and for some reason, to smell him. She always loved the way dogs smelled.

"That's enough," a masculine voice said from behind her. "Maybe you'd better get away while the getting's good."

Pressley gave Jasper one last scratch behind the ears and he tilted his head appreciatively. "Good boy," she said and slowly rose to her feet. This time, when she turned around, she saw the most handsome man she'd ever set eyes on.

~ Two ~

Janet, who'd been quiet as the proverbial church mouse, something Pressley could already tell was uncharacteristic of her new boss, finally spoke. "This is Hayden." Janet's eyes narrowed with the introduction as if she were trying to send Pressley a warning. But it wasn't necessary — Hayden and Jasper were off limits: that she already knew.

Pressley gave Hayden an unsure smile. She wasn't a good judge of character when it came to people — at least not as good as she was with animals. She had a feel for animals, mostly for dogs, but humans were a puzzle, especially the male of the species. Hayden smiled back despite her lukewarm greeting. His eyes were pale blue and crinkled at the sides. And was that a pair of dimples beneath the dark blond beard? Pressley was fascinated by his head of shaggy hair. It wasn't styled, exactly, yet with every movement, it fell perfectly back into place. She noticed his large, masculine hands, and when he pushed up his sleeves, she spotted muscled forearms and imagined that the rest of him must be built just as formidably. She felt her face flush for the second time that day and quickly reined in her thoughts.

"He seems to like me," Pressley said to Hayden while gesturing toward Jasper.

Hayden laughed. "He doesn't like anyone, sweetie. I'm afraid this boy is beyond rehabilitation. Rescued from a dog-fighting ring. Sad story."

Janet took Pressley by the arm and gave it a good yank, but Pressley stood her ground. Never mind the warning, she thought. She was intrigued by both man and dog. "Pressley," she said to Hayden, offering a hand. He took it without breaking eye contact and gave it a firm shake. She liked that. He wasn't one of those guys who treated her differently because she was a woman, though the pet name, 'sweetie' had given her pause.

"First day?" he asked.

Pressley nodded. From behind her, she heard Janet sigh and then the click of her heels as she left. First hour on the job and she was already in trouble. She wondered if she'd still be employed when she went back to the office.

"Who do I talk to about adopting Jasper?"

Hayden's expression darkened. "You can't. He's not up for adoption. Besides, you'd be a fool to take a dog like this."

"He likes me. Watch." Pressley turned to Jasper, and without hesitation, put her hand back through the bars. Jasper growled, and Hayden grabbed her by the shoulders, pulling her out of danger a split second before the dog's jaws clamped down.

"Told you. He's unpredictable. It's sad, but that's life, isn't it? Not everyone or everything is fortunate enough to have a good start in life."

Pressley's heart beat triple time — was it from his touch or because she almost lost a hand? "I'm sorry. I was just petting him not five minutes ago and he was perfectly fine."

"Yes, I saw that." Pressley was carried away by his voice. It was deep and manly. "Don't sweat it." He smiled, and she saw that indeed, he was the owner of a pair of dimples. "Wanna see the cats? They're a wild bunch of rascals. You might go home with a few scratches, but I guarantee you they're safer than Jasper."

She shook her head. "I'd better get back to work. I've got a feeling Janet isn't happy with me."

"I bet she's not happy that we're having a conversation either. She's protective of me."

Although curious about the dynamic between Janet and Hayden, Pressley didn't have the courage to delve deeper.

"It was lovely to meet you, Hayden." She shook his hand again and cringed inwardly. Why did she always sound like a schoolmarm? She was young — not some middle-aged cat lady, then again, look where she worked. Oh God, was that her future? She could see it now, one look at the kittens and she'd melt. Soon, she'd be bringing them home! She pushed the thoughts away. Stay in the here and now, she told herself. It was a trick her therapist had taught her to quell anxiety. She took a few deep breaths, too.

"You all right?"

Pressley opened her eyes. She must look exactly how she felt, like a woman on the verge of a panic attack. She waved a hand in front of her face and took another deep breath. "I'm fine. Just hot in here. Gotta go now."

As she walked away, she knew how she must have looked to Hayden — like some crazy woman. With each step toward the safety of the office, she felt better, though still embarrassed. She thought of Janet's words. Was she right? Did she did need a bit of makeup and to loosen the super-tight bun on the top of her head? She sighed. No, she was fine just the way she was. Pressley thought of the times she said those same words to her reflection in the mirror — once in the morning and again at night. Another suggestion from her therapist, but they were words she never could bring herself to actually believe.

* * * * *

Janet was at her desk, waiting with arms crossed. "What did I tell you before we went in there?" She didn't wait for an answer. "You broke both rules within the first ten minutes on the job." With a shake of her head, she pointed toward a binder sitting on Pressley's desk. "Everything you need to know to do your job is in there. Jess, the gal you're replacing, wrote it. I don't have time to train you myself so go on, get to work. Lunch is at one — you get half an hour. You might be tempted to go back in there, you know to see the animals, and I can't stop you, but please remember what I said, leave Hayden and Jasper alone."

Pressley nodded and took a seat at her desk. Though she did want to bring to Janet's attention the fact that it was her idea to go out into the back, not Pressley's. None of what just happened was her fault. Despite ignoring Janet's attempts to pull her away from Jasper and Hayden, it was Janet herself who took her over to see Jasper in the first place, and how the heck was she to know Hayden would be right there, too!

As for the binder, she slid it to the farthest corner. She didn't need anyone or anything to do her job. She may be lacking in self-esteem in some areas, but not when it came to brainy stuff. She, Pressley James, was one smart cookie, and she knew it.

* * * * *

Pressley ate lunch at her desk, deciding not to push her luck with Janet. Her job consisted of writing up blurbs for social media sites. She'd found a computer file with a list of postings, along with pictures of the animals. Each contained detailed notes on the animal's intake date and adoption date. It was an easy job, taking no time to master, and was a welcomed change from her previous career as a realtor. Something she was not cut out for. Real estate was a career for an extrovert and Pressley leaned more toward the sensitive, introverted type, though her feisty side did emerge from time to time. She never could understand why people thought extroverts were better and were always telling her she should be more outgoing. She didn't want to be anything but herself.

Despite her reserved personality, she'd managed to do well for herself in the real estate business, making a ton of money during the boom. She'd bought two small properties and rented them out for a steady income, and now that she didn't have to work for the money, she'd searched for a job more suited to her personality. Pressley loved animals and hoped that soon, she'd get to spend more time in the back, "helping out." She didn't mind cleaning — it would give her one-on-one time with the barkers and kitty cats, as Janet called them. And maybe sneak in some time with Hayden?

Just thinking of him made the heat rise in her neck and face. Pressley fanned herself cool. Janet had told her to stay away from Hayden — that he preferred to keep to himself — but that wasn't the impression she'd gotten.

Feisty girl was banging on the walls she'd built, but fear kept her jailed.

~ Three ~

Hayden Pearce picked up the framed picture on his nightstand. It was a selfie they'd taken at the cottage two summers ago. That place had been heaven on Earth, but now, Hayden had to push the sweet memories away because they'd turned sour.

It had already been a year since the accident, but it was still hard to believe Shaun was gone. He spoke aloud all the time, hoping that somewhere, somehow, Shaun could hear him. Was his fiancée watching from wherever it is we go when we die? He doubted it, because if there was a world beyond the physical, with a god of some sort, it didn't make sense that the person he loved would be so cruelly snatched away three months before their wedding.

He sat heavily on the bed and thumbed away tears. He replaced the picture, gave his head a good shake and silently scolded himself for indulging in self-pity. What's in the past cannot be undone. He had to soldier on if he was to bring Shaun's dreams to fruition — that meant working at the shelter to find permanent homes for the animals.

The day, however, hadn't been a total disappointment. The new woman, Pressley, was nice enough, and attractive in a sexy librarian kind of way. Her cheekbones were high and angular, her eyes kind, and her lips full. He was surprised with how much he'd noticed about her. The fact that Jasper *almost* seemed to like her buoyed his spirits. He'd been working at the shelter since it opened. It was something he and Shaun did together, and in all that time, not one animal had been put down unless it was old or sick. Jasper was young, probably only two or three years old. He sighed. There was no reason to cling to hope. Jasper was on his way to that rainbow bridge where all animals eventually wind up.

Shaun though, would have been torn up about Jasper. After all, her family owned the shelter. The Westons were animal lovers and philanthropists. Yet, once Shaun died, the family fell away from both him and the shelter — both were painful reminders of a life cut short, he realized, and even though it hurt, Hayden was determined to keep Shaun's dreams alive.

He cleared away leftover Chinese food from his desk and sat down. He wasn't much of a computer guy but from time to time, he checked out Facebook and played a few games online. Hours later, with sleep-heavy eyes, he powered off his laptop. It was time to turn in. A new day would be dawning soon enough.

Each day blurred into the next with nothing much changing. Even weekends were uneventful, and so he filled them with working around the house — anything to take his mind off his broken heart. Yet tonight, something inside him, some tiny niggling of excitement, flickered. Could Pressley be responsible for that? She looked to be near his age — maybe just a year or two younger, but compared to Janet and the volunteers, she was a breath of fresh air. And God knew he could use a friend right now. He'd been a hermit far too long.

And, if he was honest with himself, he was curious to see if what Pressley said about Jasper was true. Had the dog really taken to her? He'd missed most of that interaction, but he did see Pressley petting the dog. That was major despite what happened the second time she tried. But the dog lunging like that might have been because *he* was there with Pressley. Jasper didn't like men. He let out a sigh. Grief was messing with his head. Finding a home for Jasper was just wishful thinking.

But then why wouldn't the notion leave him? Hayden pondered — Pressley did say she wanted to adopt the dog. It was all her idea. What would it hurt to get the two of them together again so he could watch their interaction? Maybe Jasper wasn't as far gone as everyone thought. He owed it to Shaun to try.

Hayden pulled off his jeans and T-shirt, headed to the bathroom to brush his teeth and when he looked at his reflection, he saw the bags under his eyes, the shaggy hair and beard. He'd let himself go. He opened a drawer and took out a pair of scissors, his electric razor, shaving cream and a couple disposal razors. He was going to need the full arsenal to clean himself up properly. He'd have a bit of a five o'clock shadow by morning, but it would be a big improvement on how he looked like right now.

When he was done with his beard, he trimmed his hair down until it was a manageable length for the electric trimmer. Hayden set the trimmer to the longest length

— he didn't want to scalp himself — and then he got to work. When he was done, he barely recognized himself. Looking back at him was the *before* version of Hayden. If Shaun were looking down on him, he was sure she would be pleased.

He jumped into bed and looked over at the picture. "I miss you." He reached out a finger and lightly touched the photo. Tears begin again, but he willed them away — one day the pain would subside. It was already getting easier, wasn't it? Even if just a little?

~ Four ~

Pressley worked up the nerve to bring in her own laptop. She didn't know if Janet would approve and she was already walking a fine line with the woman, but oh man, work was soooooo much better with her trusty Mac Book Pro. She hauled the old monitor off her desk, found a corner of the office to tuck it away in, and settled the slim, powerful machine on the worn veneer. Then she grabbed the bottle of Windex and a roll of paper towel and got to work cleaning the office. She was done by the time Janet walked in.

Her boss didn't notice the Mac Book or Pressley's cleaning job. Or, maybe Janet just didn't care. Either way, Pressley was happy. Her nose no longer tickled, and she'd be able to type faster and navigate the Internet on her own laptop.

*****

Pressley finished a full day's work before lunch. A thought jumped to mind, or maybe it was more of an urge. She powered off her Mac Book and announced, "I'm gonna go out back. Maybe clean out some cages. That okay?"

Janet swiveled round in her chair and with narrowed eyes, took a long, slow, breath and let it out in a huff. "You finish all your postings for the day already?"

Pressley nodded.

"Guess I can't stop you. Cleaning up in back is part of the job, too."

She swiveled back around and when Pressley passed her on her way out, she noticed Janet was engrossed in a game of Candy Crush, volume set to mute.

Last Chances

When she opened the heavy metal door and heard the barks, whimpers, and meows, she relaxed despite the prospect of running into Hayden, which would surely make her heart somersault. But this was why she was here — for the animals. They were her true love. She needed to familiarize herself with the shelter area of the building, so she took a left and made her way to where the cats were housed. She stopped to watch a pile of kittens playing. They were too busy with each other to bother with her — jumping and pouncing, and batting each other.

While the kittens played, she opened the cage door and fished out a litter box, quickly closing it again before they realized freedom lay just steps away. Pressley searched through cupboards until she found clean litter and garbage bags. She made quick work of the smelly job, replacing the clean box and then moved on to filling the food bowls. This brought the kittens pouncing over. Their barely audible meows made her smile. She reached in and snagged a calico, closing the door behind it. She held it close to her chest and snuggled her face against it, enjoying the soft warmth of its body. The tiny fluff ball sniffed her and began to knead her sweater, its claws plucking up threads, but she didn't care. She closed her eyes for a moment and listened to the faint purring become louder as the kitten made itself comfortable.

A little orange fella pressed itself against the cage, wanting some attention, too. Pressley petted it with as many fingers as she could fit through the bars. Soon, another identical kitten sauntered over for a little affection and before she could stop herself, Pressley had the door open and was on the floor playing with all five of them. The calico remained curled in a neat ball on her lap. Maybe kittens *were* her thing after all.

She doled out kisses and cuddles before corralling the kittens back into their cage and heading off to the one next door, where she did the same thing — cleaned litter boxes, filled water and food bowls, dished out kisses and cuddles, then moved on to the next, and the next, and the next. Pressley cleaned and tidied and petted as many as she could, but the cages of cats seemed never ending. The sheer volume of animals in the place made her marvel at how the shelter managed to find homes for so many.

She silently chided herself for not cleaning all the cages. She'd intended to and knew she'd score brownie points with Janet if she had, but the cats were too cute not to spend time cuddling. A few were shy and a few hissed when she neared, but she had a feeling they'd warm to her in time. That is if they were at the shelter long enough. At every opportunity Janet boasted about the quick turnaround in finding "forever" homes for the furry residents, and then hinted that the turnaround rate might even improve now that they had Pressley working the social media campaigns. Pressley certainly hoped so, and was determined to do her best.

So far, she'd managed not to run into Hayden, but curiosity had her eying the long hallway. Was he down there? He might be right around that corner. The thought made her heart race. Maybe she should get back to the office. She checked her cell phone for the time. It was only three and she'd already eaten her leftover casserole at her desk. What else could she do with her day? She decided to stick with the cats for a while longer — no dogs, no matter how tempted she was — just visit a few more fluffballs and then back to the office.

The kennels in the feline area were smaller, so she had a better sight line in case Hayden headed her way. But what would she do if he did? Scamper away like a scared schoolgirl? No, she thought not. She'd face him. She'd talk to him, despite Janet's warning and her own anxieties.

She was holding a brown tabby, a full-grown male with a sweet, laid-back disposition, when she heard him.

"That's Sam. He's one of our long-time residents. Probably won't find a home for this fella." Hayden scratched behind Sam's ears. "Sometimes I let him out of his cage to roam the place. He's like a dog, follows me around. When the time comes to put him back in his kennel, he goes willingly. I don't know why no one has snatched him up. He'd be the perfect pet."

For an instant, she hadn't recognized him. Without the beard and shaggy mane, Hayden could pass for a college student. It was his voice that gave him away. Even though she'd barely spoken to him, she'd know it anywhere.

"Maybe I should do a feature on him? On our site?" Pressley suggested. "We might find someone to take him." She tried to keep the wobble from her voice. Hayden's sudden presence gave her no time to prepare and her heart jackhammered against her rib cage.

Hayden held out his arms for the cat and Pressley handed Sam over. "This might sound selfish, but I kinda like having this guy around. He keeps me company." Hayden bent to let Sam down and once his paws hit the floor, he wound around Hayden's legs and purred.

"I think he's yours already." She laughed.

Hayden smiled. There were those dimples again, but this time she got the full show. "Don't tell Sam, but I'm more of a dog person," he whispered and then was quick to hold up a stilling hand. "I love cats too, but there's nothing like a good dog, ya know? They're loyal and you can take 'em on hikes and for runs in the park." He looked as if he was lost in a sweet memory.

"So, you have a dog?" Pressley asked.

"No. Not right now."

She was surprised and wanted to ask the obvious — why hadn't he adopted one of the scores of dogs at the shelter? He must have a few favorites. Even she was on the lookout for a potential pet.

"Shaun and I had a Boston terrier a while ago. Name was Roxy." He looked at the floor, seemingly examining his workbooks, and when he looked back up at her, she thought she saw the glint of tears in his eyes.

"I'm sorry. I didn't mean to upset you." The name Shaun bounced around in her brain. Was he gay?

"Don't be sorry. I'm just not used to talking about personal stuff." He waved a dismissive hand. "Anyway, that's all in the past. Maybe I'll tell you about it some day, but not today, okay?" He gave her a sad smile.

"I like your hair," she blurted and was immediately sorry. What was wrong with her?

"Yeah? It's kinda short." He ran a hand back and forth over the top of his head. "I'm not quite used to it yet. I was rockin' the mountain man look for a while."

Pressley liked that look too, but seeing more of his handsome face was better. She was relieved he was still standing in front of her, talking, and hadn't taken off yet. His sweet, crooked grin soothed her anxieties.

"Come on." He took her by the arm. "You wanna go see Jasper?"

Shock stole her words and for a moment she stood there, speechless. Hayden waved her forward. "No, I can't. Janet told me to stay away from him and ... you warned me too. Besides, the cat ... Where'd he go? Doesn't he have to be put back in his cage?"

"Sam's fine. Probably found a warm spot to curl up in for a while. He'll head back home once he's hungry."

Hayden stood in front of her and placed both hands on her shoulders. "You know

Jasper's not going to be around much longer, don't you? Dr. Graham, the vet, is coming next week."

A jolt of adrenaline shot through her. She knew Jasper's days were numbered, but not that he was to be put down that soon. Didn't Hayden realize that seeing him would only break her heart?

"Thought you'd like to pay him one last visit. He doesn't get many visitors and you said he liked you."

The abrupt turn of events was mind-boggling. Why did he want her to visit with Jasper, especially after the warnings from both himself and Janet? But how could she say no?

Jasper's ears stood at attention as Pressley neared.

"I'll stay back here. He doesn't like me much," Hayden whispered.

"Really? You're letting me see him alone?" The dog couldn't do her harm even if he wanted to. He was, after all, behind bars, and this time, she wasn't about to stick her hand through like she did before. It bothered her that Hayden was leaving her on her own, but she soldiered on.

"Hey, Jasper," she cooed, and crouched down beside the cage door. The dog got to his feet and trotted over, tail wagging. His large, muscular body banged the door as he sat leaning against it, trying to get as close to her as possible.

Jasper pressed his snout between the bars, his nose twitching to pick up her scent. He whined and pawed the concrete, as if willing Pressley closer. She held out a hand and immediately felt the cold wet of the dog's large nose against the back of her hand. He slobbered her with kisses. With confidence buoyed, she moved closer and, just as she did before, Pressley slipped her hand through the bars and scratched behind his ears. Jasper tilted his large head and shut his eyes.

Last Chances

"I know you said I couldn't, but I really want to take him home, Hayden. Can you arrange it, please?"

~ Five ~

Regret slammed Hayden like a punch to the throat. Part of him hadn't really expected his plan to work and now that it had, he was torn. On the one hand, he'd be saving Jasper's life, but on the other, he could be putting Pressley in danger. Jasper had bitten Shaun when he was first brought in, leaving a puncture mark in the space between her thumb and index finger. But that had been out of fear, he reasoned — new place, new people. The poor dog was just protecting himself.

Besides, Jasper really did like Pressley; maybe she was the right person for him. Whatever it was that she had, or was doing — her soft voice, her gentle demeanor, the kindness that oozed from her — Jasper had picked up on it.

Last Chances

Hayden's thoughts ping-ponged — was he pushing the dog on Pressley because Shaun would have wanted Jasper saved, or was he respecting Pressley's wishes?

He could bear it no longer. Guilt made him speak. "Maybe you should think about it for a day or two before jumping into something that might be more trouble than it's worth."

"But he's supposed to be put down next week, right?"

"Yeah, but that gives you some time to think about it. And, it'll give you time to soften up Janet about adopting Jasper. She'll flip out when she finds out you want him."

Pressley got to her feet and stretched out her back. She looked thoughtful, then finally nodded her assent. "Couldn't hurt, I guess but please make sure you'll watch over him. The vet won't come in early to put him down, right?"

"No, don't worry. I'll make sure he won't."

Pressley looked at the wall clock. "I have to get back to work. Janet's probably wondering what I'm up to."

"Wait! Um, maybe we should talk about this whole Jasper thing a bit more. I know quite a bit about his history," Hayden said. "Might help you make up your mind."

"I really should get back to the office, Hayden."

"No, I didn't mean right now. I meant after work. I'll come by your place to pick you up. Maybe we could grab a bite, or something?" Hayden felt his checks flush. It was not something he was used to. In fact, he hadn't felt this way since he was in high school. What was it about this plain Jane that stirred him? Maybe it was that she really wasn't such a plain Jane after all. He saw beneath the façade. Those big brown eyes, full lips, and thick dark hair she kept in a bun.

More than anything he wanted to see what it looked like cascading over her shoulders. Pressley was a beautiful woman, despite her best efforts at hiding her assets.

Her eyes widened and for a moment, Hayden was afraid she wasn't going to answer. Again, her eyes darted to the clock. "Um, yeah, that would be fine, I guess."

Hayden pulled out his phone and smiled with relief, though he wished she'd been more enthusiastic in her response. "Wanna give me your address and number?"

"Can we meet?" Pressley said.

"Huh?"

"Can we meet at the place? Wherever it is you want to grab a bite?"

Hayden's smile faded. "Um, sure. Six o'clock good for you, or is it too early? We can meet at Cranbrook Park and take it from there." He wanted to add, "It's a busy, public place, so you'll feel safe." His pride was wounded, but he'd survive and besides, he couldn't really blame her for being cautious; after all, they'd only just met.

She took his phone and punched in her number, leaving blank the space where an address would go, then handed it back. "Text me your number so I'll have it in case I'm running late, okay?"

* * * * *

Pressley left work promptly at 4:30 to get ready to meet Hayden at Cranbrook Park. She was home now and in her bedroom, looking through her closet for something comfortable, yet stylish — if such an outfit even existed. It was a good idea, even at this time of year when chilly days were more frequent than warm ones, to meet at the park. It was out in the open where other people would be, not that she was scared of him. On the contrary, for some reason, she trusted him, but she was nervous to have him over to her house. Her social anxiety kicked into high gear just at the notion. If only she could call her therapist. A pep talk would do her some good right now. But they'd parted ways when they'd mutually agreed she was able to cope on her own.

She'd have to get into Hayden's car at some point, so he could take her to wherever they were going to eat — that might be uncomfortable, especially if they had nothing to talk about except Jasper.

A sudden heart-rending thought sprang to mind — what if this was actually a date? Getting together to talk about Jasper was nerve-racking but tolerable, but the notion of a date made her nauseous with fear. She made her way to her dresser mirror and leaned forward until her face was inches away. "Stop! You are good enough just the way you are. You are smart and kind and have no reason to be scared," Pressley told her reflection. This time she halfway believed herself. She remembered Hayden mentioning the name 'Shaun' — so then, what was she afraid of? He was probably gay and really did just want to talk about Jasper. He'd said he knew quite a bit about the dog. That had to be it! She took in a deep breath and let it out slowly. After a few more, her pulse slowed, and her stomach settled.

Back to her closet she went, grabbed a pair of jeans and a sweater and, after changing, she was in front of her mirror again, this time to inspect her bun. It was in its usual neat pile atop her head. She reached for the bobby pins and hair ties holding it in place and began to pull them out. She stopped. Her bun was a leaning wobble on the verge of collapsing. Was she really going to let her hair down? She smiled at her reflection. "Yes, I am," she proclaimed and with expert fingers, pulled the last of the snag-free hair elastics out, along with the remaining pins. She brushed out the knots. It felt great not to be so confined. Her usual routine was to put her hair in a ponytail once she got home; very rarely did she ever let it hang loose. But now that the pressure of a date was gone, she wanted to be comfortable.

After donning a pair of hoop earrings and applying a little lipstick, she was ready to go.

~ Six ~

The light was waning, but the park was brightly lit and for an evening in November in South Carolina, the weather was surprisingly warm. She texted Hayden before getting out of her car. She should have asked him what he drove, but it was too late now.

He didn't text back. He didn't have to. She saw him sauntering over after jumping from the driver's seat of a black pickup truck, a big smile on his face.

"Hey, you hungry?" he said when he got to her window.

Unsure of whether to get out of her car, Pressley simply nodded. Hayden opened the car door and moved out of the way for her. "All right, come on, then."

She killed the engine and grabbed her purse. Before following, she chirped the car alarm and checked the door to make sure it was locked, then she zipped up her coat.

Instead of getting into the truck, Hayden opened the tailgate, hopped up and held out a hand for Pressley. Behind him, she saw a cooler and blankets. She was completely bewildered but took his hand nonetheless.

He pulled her up and she landed in the bed of the truck with an inelegant thud.

Hayden laughed. "Sorry, I didn't mean to pull so hard."

Pressley felt the heat of embarrassment rise in her cheeks, and laughed to cover her feelings. Hayden helped her to her feet and smiled contritely. "You okay? Didn't hurt anything, did you?"

She shook her head no. The plastic cargo liner had softened her landing.

"Great!" He turned around and she heard rummaging. "This is a little unconventional, but I wanted to do something different," he called over his shoulder. When he turned back around, she was presented with a low-slung, canvas chair complete with a cup holder in the armrest. Hayden set one up for himself as well.

"Go ahead — have a seat. I'll set up dinner."

She'd never eaten dinner in the back of a pickup before; hell, she'd never even been in the back of a pickup. But relief settled in with the realization she and Hayden weren't going to a restaurant after all. It was unconventional, but more than that, it was simple, and Pressley was all about that.

Hayden set a small table in front of them. It wasn't much larger than a TV tray and it sparked childhood memories of the times her mom let her eat dinner in front of the television, so they could watch sitcoms together. He placed a small plastic tablecloth over it and smoothed it flat.

"We barely know each other, so I apologize in advance if I've picked food you don't like," Hayden said as he opened the cooler. "I don't have a picnic basket." He laughed.

"A cooler will do in a pinch," Pressley replied. She had to admit she was amused and was curious about what Hayden's idea of picnic food would be.

He took out a bottle of red wine and two plastic cups and placed them on the table, followed by sandwiches wrapped in tinfoil.

"Everyone likes wine, right?" He uncorked the bottle, poured the wine, then handed her a glass.

She did like wine, especially red, and was grateful to have something to calm her nerves. But he's gay, she suddenly remembered — nothing to be nervous about. The thought didn't have its intended effect — yes, it did calm her, but it also made her heart heavy.

"And, since I chose a Chianti, I figured meatball sandwiches would be a nice accompaniment. Italian food — a safe choice, right?" Before she could answer, he nodded toward the cooler. "I even have tiramisu for dessert."

"You went to a lot of trouble."

Hayden laughed. "Wow, you're low maintenance if you think sitting in the back of a truck eating meatball sandwiches is a lot of trouble." He picked up her sandwich and slid a paper plate under it. "Now I feel bad that I didn't bring real plates."

She sipped her wine and unwrapped her sandwich. They ate and drank and did their best to fill in the silences with small talk. She wondered when the topic of Jasper was going to be broached. Should she be the one to bring him up, or let Hayden take the lead?

She decided to wait. The evening was young, and he *was* doing his best to be hospitable. Hayden would eventually fill her in on Jasper as he'd promised. She just had to be patient. After another glass of wine, the chitchat came easier, the wine having transported her to blissful laxity.

By the time they'd finished dessert, the sun had been replaced by a full moon. That and the lights around the perimeter of the parking lot cast a cozy glow.

Hayden made quick work of the cleanup by throwing everything into a plastic grocery bag. "You warm enough?" he asked. "I have blankets."

Pressley shook her head. She was perfectly content — her belly was full, and her head was just cloudy enough to whisk away all worry. It also gave her the courage to study his face, without turning away every time their eyes met. The lighting was complimentary and made his jawline unapologetically masculine. His lips were full and totally kissable. If only he were straight!

As Hayden tied the handles of the plastic bag, readying it for the garbage can, he said, "So, I went through Jasper's records today. He's been in the shelter a little over a year and although I remember the day he was brought in and the reasons why, I wanted to make sure I wasn't missing anything. You need to know everything about him before deciding whether to adopt him."

Pressley perked up. Here it was, the conversation she'd been waiting for. She was grateful for his consideration. Yes, it was important to know as much as possible about the dog so that she could provide the best home possible for him. It didn't matter what he was going to say, she'd already made up her mind that Jasper would be hers. She'd dog-proof the house, arrange to have someone come by to let him out and take him for a walk. Luckily, she had those resources at her fingertips — there was a bulletin board filled with business cards for all kinds of doggie daycares and professional dog walkers at the shelter.

"You wanna walk and talk?" He held up the plastic bag. "Maybe find a garbage can for this?"

Pressley was up for a walk. She stood, zipped her coat up as far as possible, and donned a pair of black knit gloves. She was nothing if not prepared for any eventuality. She even had a pair of earmuffs in her purse but thought better of fishing them out. If worse came to worst, the hood of her coat would warm her enough.

Hayden jumped down and offered his hand. Pressley took it and hopped down off the tailgate with uncharacteristic grace. She was grateful to have landed so elegantly. Was Hayden impressed?

She was already familiar with the park and the walking paths, though she'd only visited in the summers. After disposing of their litter, Hayden took the lead and chose the path that bordered the lake.

"Correct me if I'm wrong, but I think I've already told you Jasper was in a dog-fighting ring, right? His owner was arrested and charged. He went to jail for two months and was fined five hundred dollars." Hayden shook his head. "It's disgusting — just a slap on the wrist, really. He had five dogs that he used for fighting, but Jasper was the only one in good enough shape to bring into the shelter. The other four had to be euthanized."

"That's awful. I don't understand what's wrong with this world. That monster's probably doing it again." It was hard to think about — animals being used in such a horrendous way.

"That I don't know, but Jasper was one hell of a fighter and I'm pretty sure he still is." Hayden sighed. "I have a confession to make."

Those words stopped Pressley in her tracks. She looked at Hayden, waiting.

He let loose another sigh, then began, "I've been selfish."

"What do you mean?"

He thrust his hands into his coat pockets and took a while to answer, which made Pressley's heart beat a little harder. What in the world was he about to say? She wanted to pull the words from him.

Finally, he spoke. "Finding a home for Jasper was Shaun's greatest wish. She loved that dog and I'm afraid I might be pushing him on you just to keep my promise to her. I'm not sure taking Jasper is the right thing to do."

Was it the fact he'd just said "her" and "she" or that he was trying to talk her out of taking the dog that made her flush? Pressley spotted a nearby bench and made a beeline for it.

Hayden followed and sat beside her. "What are you thinking? You disappointed?"

How could she say what she was thinking? A smile wanted to bloom on her lips and yet her heart was beating so fast, it stole her breath.

~ Seven ~

Hayden tried to read the expression on Pressley's face. She looked terrified but kind of happy at the same time. He was utterly and thoroughly confused. "Say something," he urged.

Her eyes darted up to his and then away again. She opened her mouth, moved her lips, but not a word escaped.

Pressley got up and started to walk away at a brisk pace, making him jog to catch up. He passed her and turned around, walking backwards so he could face her. "Please, Pressley. What's wrong?"

The wind had picked up and her hair whipped wildly around her face. It was cooler by the lake. Hayden did his best to shield her as she struggled to pull on her hood. Maybe the usual practical bun wouldn't have been such a bad idea this night. Or maybe she'd ditched the bun because she wanted to look nice for him. He noticed she was wearing lipstick, too, but she was beautiful even without makeup.

"Maybe I should go home," she said, finally.

"But why?"

She was busy tucking her hair into her hood. "Because it's cold and ... I don't know. I'm not feeling so great."

Hayden wrapped an arm around her. "Come on, let's go sit in my truck. We can talk there." He felt her body stiffen as he hurried her back along the path to the parking lot. Thankfully, they hadn't wandered too far away.

"I should just go," she protested.

"I'll respect your wishes, really, I will, but can I have just one more minute? Please?"

She nodded.

Once they were in the front seat of his truck, he turned the engine on and hoped it would warm up quickly. He wanted Pressley to be comfortable.

He opened the compartment between them, took out a bag and handed it to her.

"What's this?" she asked. Her hood was still on, concealing most of her face.

"I bought it for Jasper, in case you still wanted him after everything I told you. It's a muzzle. It'll keep you safe until he's adjusted to his new home."

She took it out of the bag and examined it. "It seems a bit barbaric."

"No, it won't hurt him. It'll just keep him from biting." Hayden closed his eyes and took a deep breath. Everything about this woman was a puzzle.

"I like you." The words tumbled out before he could stop them.

She turned, and he could see her face now. Slowly, he reached over and removed the hood from around her head. It was as if he was on automatic pilot as he ran a hand through her hair. Pressley closed her eyes and a small smile curled her lips. And then he kissed her.

* * * * *

For a moment, Pressley thought she was going to faint. He'd actually made her head spin, or was it the wine? Either way, the kiss thrilled her but also embarrassed her. She'd acted like a fool. Her nerves had gotten the better of her again, but Hayden's kiss had awakened that side of her she'd kept under wraps — sensuality begging to be let loose.

"That was nice," she said with a smile.

"You're beautiful," Hayden replied, and leaned in for another kiss. This one made her toes curl, and the fiery woman inside clawed her way to the surface. Pressley wrapped her arms around Hayden's

Last Chances

neck and inched as close as she could get. She didn't care that her heart beat wildly, that her breath came in hot, short rasps — she wanted him so badly, it hurt.

~ Eight ~

Hayden hadn't felt this way with any other woman since Shaun. He hadn't expected such an eruption of desire. He looked at her then, the moonlight shining off her thick, dark hair, highlighting the angles of her face, her sensual mouth. He wanted more of her, but when he slipped a hand under her coat and around her waist to pull her closer, she shook her head.

"Can we talk for a bit?"

He'd do anything to make her happy, even push his own desires to the back burner, to simmer. "Of course."

"What happened?" Pressley whispered and without asking what she meant, he answered, because he knew. He told her about Shaun, about the car accident that took her life three months before they were to be married. He told her how he struggled, how he'd gone off the deep end for a while and tried to drink away his sorrows. He told her about Shaun, too. About her ideals and love of animals and how Pressley reminded him of her.

Pressley confessed how she'd thought he was gay, making Hayden roar with laughter. "Really, do I give off that vibe?"

"No, that's why I was confused."

"But I get it. Shaun's not a typical name for a woman. Her real name was Jane and she hated it. She was a firecracker! Feisty and strong-willed. The name suited her."

"Sounds like a great woman," Pressley said, feeling a little deflated. She wasn't anything like Shaun from the sounds of it. How Hayden could say she reminded him of her was baffling, but she loved it nonetheless.

"So, what should we do now?" Hayden asked.

Pressley checked the time on the dashboard. "Maybe I should go home. Work tomorrow." She didn't know why she'd said that. The last thing she wanted was to leave this man. She wanted to stay with Hayden, to talk more, to learn about him, and of course, she wanted more of his kisses.

"I've got a better idea." Hayden threw the truck into drive and smiled when Pressley let loose with a barrage of questions. It wasn't that she was unhappy to be with him, just that surprises weren't her favorite thing. She liked to be in control and that meant knowing where he was taking her right now.

When they pulled up in front of a PetSmart five minutes later, Hayden took Pressley's hand and said, "Let's grab a few things for Jasper. He's going to need some stuff if he's being adopted." He threw her a wink.

Pressley's heart jumped for joy. "So, it's going to happen? I really am going to get Jasper?"

"Let's just say I'll do my best to make it happen, but I really wanted to tell you about Jasper's past before you decided. It made me feel better because I felt like I was forcing him on you."

"No, I want to give him a home — a real home for once in his life. You're not forcing me to do anything. I admit that I'm nervous. It'll take some time before Jasper and I are comfortable with each other, but I really think everything will be fine," Pressley said. "So then, Janet's on board?"

Hayden took a breath and let it out slowly. "No, that's one of the road blocks we're facing, but don't worry, I'll convince her. I have no worries about that and neither should you. There are a few legal obstacles to get past, but hey, look where we are." He pointed to the store. "Let's go get Jasper some nice new things. My treat."

* * * * *

Pressley was back in her car and on her way home. Her back seat stuffed with food, treats, a doggie bed and other necessities every dog owner needed. She'd said her goodbyes to Hayden in the parking lot at the park. Another long, lovely kiss, followed by a hug she never wanted to end.

That evening, Pressley would go to bed still drunk on the lingering feel of Hayden's lips on hers and the warmth of his body as he'd pulled her close. It had been a long time since Pressley had been kissed and something had been awakened. Her therapist would have been proud of her, and if she was still seeing him, she was sure he would be happy for her, too.

~ Nine ~

"Are you out of your mind?" Janet said when Pressley walked through the door the next morning. The small woman stood with her hands firmly planted on her hips. "You want to adopt Jasper? That dog will rip you to pieces, or if not you, someone else. He's a lost cause, hon." When she saw Pressley's smile fade Janet's expression changed from shock to sorrow. "Don't get me wrong, I feel bad too, and when I first started here way back when, I wanted to take home every single one of them pups and kitties."

Pressley had steeled herself for Janet's protestations, but couldn't help to defend her position. "I'm adopting the dog, Janet. Hayden said it was fine. I've got everything set up at my place. I even have a muzzle for him until he gets used to his new home. Plus, I took down a few names and numbers from the bulletin board. I'm going to arrange for his care during the day when I'm at work. It's all covered."

Pressley walked over to her desk and plopped into her chair. It rolled away and as if it had a mind of its own, and even turned her around so she wasn't facing Janet.

The sound of people whispering turned her back around. Pressley saw Hayden standing inside the office door, just a foot away from Janet. He gave her a smile and a wave. Then he stepped into the office and sat on the corner of Janet's desk.

Janet held up a stilling hand and shook her head. "Don't bother trying to talk me into it, Hayden. Jasper's more dog than she can handle. And, you don't have to tell me how we're a no-kill shelter and how it's our mission to do everything in our power to find homes for all our animals."

Suddenly, his face was a thundercloud. "And to keep the ones we can't find homes for, here at the shelter," Hayden finished. "Have you forgotten about Jasper's appointment with Dr. Graham next week?"

"I would keep him, if I could! That would be the one and only option we'd have for that dog, but he's not a candidate." Janet's voice dropped to a whisper. "Jasper bit Shaun, remember? I know you do. Three stitches, Hayden, remember? You want that to happen to Pressley, too?"

"Hey, I'm right here," Pressley interjected. "Can I be part of this conversation?"

Hayden turned to her. "Sorry, of course you can."

"Is that true? About Jasper biting Shaun?" Pressley asked.

Janet's eyes widened. "She knows about Shaun? My oh my, things are happening faster than the speed of light around here!"

Hayden nodded. "Yes, I told her." He turned to Pressley. "Jasper bit her the day he was rescued and brought here. He was scared, not vicious but ever since then, he's been labeled a dangerous animal."

"And you don't think he is?" Janet asked. "Maybe we should go on out back and see if he'll let you pet him."

"You know he dislikes men," Hayden said. "He comes by that mistrust naturally. Can't blame the poor animal."

"Well, I wouldn't be sticking my hand in the cage to give him a scratch behind the ears any time soon," Janet said.

Hayden sighed in frustration. "Call the family, see what they say. They own this place. It'll have to be their decision."

Janet's lips pursed to a thin line as she eyed Hayden. It looked as if there was going to be a standoff when Hayden abruptly turned and began to walk away. "We'll talk later," he called over his shoulder.

Once the door at the end of the hall slammed, Janet turned to Pressley and narrowed her eyes. Pressley noticed the shimmer of Janet's blue eye shadow and tried not to wince at what was coming.

"You've been here less than a week and all hell's breaking loose over that dog," Janet protested.

"Jasper likes me, Janet. He let me pet him twice now and both you and Hayden know that's not like him. What if I just take him home for a day or two and see what happens?"

Janet wagged a finger, opened her mouth to protest but thought better of it. "Look, I have to call the Westons: Shaun's family. They own this place and a lot of other places around town, too. They're richer than God but at least they're doing some good with their money. They keep us adequately funded, but I suspect there'll be legal ramifications if we let you take a dog out of here with behavioral problems." A slow smile blossomed on her face, and Pressley was taken aback.

"What?" she asked.

"I've never seen Hayden like this, at least not for one heck of a long time," Janet said.

"Like what?"

Janet sat and clasped her hands in her lap. "Remember what I told you on your first day?"

"You mean about how I shouldn't take it personally if Hayden doesn't speak to me?" Pressley said.

Janet tapped the tip of her nose with her pointer finger. "Bingo! He keeps to himself. It's unusual for him to even wander from the back room out here to the office, let alone speak up on anyone's behalf. You must have made quite an impression on him. And don't think I didn't notice how he looked at you.

Don't tell me you and Hayden went on a date?"

Pressley bit her lip to keep from smiling.

Janet looked around and then her voice dropped to a conspiratorial tone. "He's a complicated guy — always was in some ways, but since Shaun's death, he clammed up real good. That was a little over a year ago and he hasn't been the same since, understandably so, *but* if he likes you, take it from me, that's a mighty big deal. I'd grab on tight if I were you. Men like him don't come around every day."

She put a hand on Pressley's shoulder. "You know how I feel about you taking Jasper." She sighed. "But, you may not just be saving that dog, you might be saving Hayden, too. All I ask is that you be careful with him. He's still fragile."

This time, Pressley did smile. "I wouldn't hurt him, Janet. Not for the world."

"I've got a phone call to make," her boss said as she plucked up the receiver of the phone on her desk. "I don't like it one bit, but let's see what the Westons have to say about letting you adopt Jasper. They've got the final say after all."

~ Ten ~

"I can't get a hold of anyone just yet. I left a message," Janet said.

"I never thought adopting a dog would be so difficult," Pressley replied.

"It's not usually like this. Jasper's a special case. We need to cover all the bases."

Pressley was well aware of what that meant — they had to make sure they couldn't be sued if Jasper attacked anyone, and she was included in that group.

Pressley busied herself with work to keep her mind off the impending call from the Westons, but each time the phone rang, she looked over at Janet expectantly only to be disappointed. Once lunchtime rolled around, she decided to go out back to the kennels to visit with Jasper.

She heard him jump to his feet and let out a whine as she rounded the corner. Had he picked up her scent? When he saw her, his tail motored back and forth, and he eagerly stuck his nose through the bars of the cage. Pressley spoke softly, calling his name and telling him he was a good boy. She petted him as best she could through the bars, wishing she could let him out. She knew that would be crazy, yet she wanted so much to *really* pet him, and kiss the top of his head. The cage was padlocked and even if it wasn't, she wouldn't have dared open it.

She spied a chewed-up rope toy and an empty bowl in Jasper's cage. Although she couldn't play with him, she could feed him. She made her way to the cupboard where the kibble was kept and poured some into a plastic baggie, then she sat on the floor in front of the cage and dropped a few pieces through the bars. Jasper snatched them up greedily and stared at her for more. This time, she fed him by hand and to her delight, he took the kibble gently, and even licked her fingers in appreciation. She fed him until the baggie was empty. He was a smart dog and seemed to understand when there was no more food to be had. He lay on the floor beside her, inching as close as he could possibly get. She spoke to him again, eliciting more tail wags and kisses. The time she spent with Jasper solidified her decision to adopt him. If only the Westons would call. They were the only obstacles in the way.

* * * * *

When she got home, Pressley looked over Jasper's stuff, rearranging it, and putting his bed in the coziest corner of the family room. She threw a fluffy blanket on the sofa, she wasn't the kind to forbid animals on the furniture, and although she'd set another dog bed on the floor beside her bed, she wouldn't kick him out if he wanted to snuggle with her. She did, however, have a crate but would only use it as a last resort.

She'd made calls to the dog sitters from the car on her way home, and after speaking with a few, was confident Jasper would be well taken care of while she was at work. She was careful to only contact women and made appointments for a few of them to stop over on the weekend just to make sure Jasper would be fine with them. She thought of the muzzle Hayden had given her — maybe it would be a good idea to muzzle him before she left for work, she thought. The sitter could take it off him once he was safely in his crate. There was a small window in the front of it, just large enough to get a hand through. All Jasper's sitter had to do was hit the quick release on the side of the muzzle and it would be off. No harm, no foul.

She'd do it until he got used to the new routine, and the sitter. After a while she'd allow him his freedom while she ran errands, just for short periods of time until she knew she could trust him not to damage the house. Then, when both woman and dog were comfortable, no more crating and no more muzzle. Pressley had no idea how long all this would take, but she did have dogs growing up and was familiar with training them.

Her mind turned to Hayden and their date the night before. Even though they'd exchanged numbers, she hadn't heard from him. And, to make matters worse, she'd only seen him for a few minutes at work. A rush of anxiety flooded her making her snatch up her phone to check it. What if she'd missed his calls or texts? Or worse, what if he *hadn't* called or texted? A click on the home button flashed only notices from Facebook and Twitter on the screen. There were no missed calls and no texts from Hayden.

"Okay, take a deep breath," she told herself and made her way to the mirror over her dresser. "You're fine, Pressley. Hayden likes you. He wouldn't have kissed you if he didn't," she told her reflection, only she didn't fully believe it. Maybe last night's kiss was a heat of the moment type of thing. Or, maybe it was the wine! She pulled in a few deeps breaths, letting them out slowly. She tried again. "Stop it!" she said more adamantly, not letting her imagination run wild. "You always make mountains out of mole hills. Everything's fine." But then, where was he today at work? Was he hiding from her? No, she told herself — he was probably just busy; besides, if she was worried, she could always text him. But her intuition shot back a firm "no." It would be better if he contacted her. She didn't want to seem too eager. Damn but she wished she was still seeing her therapist. She needed him right now.

Pressley did the only thing she could think of to get over the panic. She put on her coat and went for a long walk. Then busied herself with other tasks until the day was over.

* * * * *

The phone startled Pressley awake. It was Janet — she was already at the shelter — the Westons had given their permission for her to adopt Jasper.

Pressley dressed quickly and ran out of the house not even bothering with breakfast. She was at the shelter an hour before she was supposed to start but it was all for a great reason — soon, Jasper would be hers. Before exiting the car, she sat for a while in the shelter's parking lot, cell phone in hand. Should she call Hayden? She scanned the parking lot for his truck and spotted it. She hovered a finger over the call button, but thought better of it. With a deep breath and chin thrust high in false bravado, she made her way into the shelter.

Hayden and Janet were waiting for her in the office, both with huge smiles on their faces. She couldn't help but smile too as relief washed over her. Once again, it appeared she'd overreacted.

Hayden spoke first. "We've got all Jasper's stuff ready, not that he had much, just his collar and a chew toy." He handed her a bag. Her hand shook as she reached for it.

Janet moved in for a hug. "I didn't think the Westons would agree but, here we are! They were happy to hear we'd found Jasper a forever home."

"Dr. Graham is out back with Jasper now. Let's go get him," Hayden suggested.

Pressley's heart skipped a beat. "Why's the vet here?"

"Relax, he's here to help with Jasper," Hayden said with a laugh. "You ready to take your new best friend home?"

When they got to Jasper's cage, the door was swung wide and Dr. Graham was bent down, fastening a leash to the dog's collar. Pressley stopped in her tracks, half expecting the dog to lunge and sink his teeth into the vet's arm, but nothing happened. Dr. Graham looked up when he noticed the trio. "Hey!" He stood. "I've got Jasper all prepped and ready." He waved Pressley over and handed her the leash. Jasper trotted out and lay by her feet.

"I gave him a mild sedative. It'll wear off in a few hours. Jasper's had a tough life. Good news is that he likes women more than men and from what I've heard, he's really taken to you. I've got a list with a few pointers for you." He reached behind him and grabbed a sheet of paper off the counter. "You're a brave and kind soul to be taking Jasper home, but please be careful with him. Read what I've written down for you and don't hesitate to call if you need me. Oh, and you'll need these." He handed her a bottle of pills. "For the first few days, give him one pill twice a day. Wrap it in a piece of cheese or meat. He'll wolf it down." The doctor noticed Pressley's apprehension and added, "It's just until he gets used to his new life and routine. He's high strung and doesn't take well to change."

Pressley nodded. This was all happening so fast. It was only when she felt the tug of the leash that she remembered Jasper was on the other end. She knelt beside him. Pressley scratched behind his ears knowing how he liked it. Big brown eyes opened and looked up at her. He moved slowly to a sitting position and plopped his large head onto her thigh. She kissed him and wrapped an arm around his thick neck and shoulders. When she rested her head against him, Pressley heard a collective intake of air from Janet, Hayden and Dr. Graham.

"Careful. Go slow," Dr. Graham cautioned and quickly added, "I'm sure he's fine though. The sedatives will have calmed him."

Hayden chimed in, "What if, well … what if when the pill wears off, he gets aggressive?"

Dr. Graham pursed his lips and shook his head. "That's the sixty-four-thousand-dollar question, now isn't it? We got to wait to see how Jasper adapts to his new life. It's not that he won't change or can't change, it's that most people aren't brave enough to give a dog with a history of behavioral problems a second chance. To be honest, I have my reservations, but Pressley is a rare breed just like your Shaun was." Dr. Graham gulped audibly making Pressley wonder if he was just as brave a soul as she was for broaching the subject of Shaun.

"Before you go, hon, there's some paperwork in the office you have to fill out. It won't take long and then you and your new baby can go home and get acquainted," Janet said. "Wanna go do that now? You can have the rest of the day off." She smiled sweetly but

Pressley had the impression her boss wanted her, and Jasper gone. Although she could tell Janet was happy for Jasper, she seemed nervous with the dog out of its cage.

The paperwork turned out to be legal documents, but she'd been expecting that. They were designed to absolve the Westons and the Paws and Claws Animal Shelter from any liability if 'said dog' became aggressive toward not just Pressley but anyone else including other animals. By this point, Pressley just wanted to sign on the many dotted lines and get home. Jasper, for his part, lay lazily at her feet, his head resting on top of her feet.

Once she was done, Janet and Dr. Graham waved from the door of the shelter while Hayden accompanied her to the car.

"You're not afraid of him right now, are you?" she asked.

"He's doped up. Bet he's happy as a clam." Hayden even dared to pet the dog. "You scared? I mean, this is a big deal. Did we get everything you need? We didn't forget anything, did we?"

"I've got two beds, toys, bowls, a crate, and a bag of food. What else could I possibly need?" Pressley couldn't hide the wobble in her voice. She was a little scared, but more than that, she was nervous to be so close to Hayden.

Pressley opened the hatch back of the car. "Life would be boring without a challenge, right?" She patted the inside of the car and Jasper jumped up — Hayden had to give him a boost to help him the rest of the way in, then he placed the dog's meager belongings in the back beside him and closed the door slowly, so he wouldn't be spooked.

"Can I see your phone?" Hayden asked.

Pressley took it out of her back pocket and handed it to him. It was an unusual request. She already had his number, but there was something about Hayden that made her trust him wholeheartedly. He was like a dog himself, but in the best ways — his big soulful eyes, the feeling that he was loyal to a fault. She watched as he scrolled through her contacts and then handed the phone back. "Just wanted to make sure my number is on speed dial. Don't hesitate to call if you need anything, okay?"

She wanted to point out that Jasper would probably attack him once the pills wore off if he came anywhere near, but held her tongue and was grateful for his offer of assistance. The muzzle might come in handy after all — at least for Hayden's visits — if that ever happened. She prayed the dog would eventually get used to men, if just for that reason alone.

Pressley got into the car and rolled down the window.

"Take it easy with him," he said, leaning in on his elbows.

"I'll be fine." She smiled. She was excited to show Jasper his new home, but not happy to be leaving Hayden. "You want to come over later?" If he hadn't been there, she would have hit her forehead with her palm. Why did she blurt things out? Was there no filter, no inner editor monitoring her thoughts so that they wouldn't become words?

Hayden glanced at Jasper sleeping in the back. "I think it's best if I stay away for a few days. He needs to get used to you and your house. You know how Jasper feels about me. But feel free to call later to let me know how it's going. And, call if … well, if things don't go as planned, okay? I'm willing to risk life and limb to help out." He smiled.

He kissed her on the forehead, right where she wanted to pound sense into herself. That one small act was enough to allay her fears. Hayden wasn't lost to her, but she'd have to rein in her insecurities or he might just run away.

~ Eleven ~

Hayden had only gone to the shelter to help Pressley with Jasper. It was his day off though he hadn't told Pressley that. It would have made her feel guilty, he reasoned. He had wanted to go with her to help with the dog, but like he'd told her, it really was best for her and Jasper to get to know each other without him in the way. Once the pills wore off, Jasper might not be happy to have his company.

He considered a hike, or even staying overnight at the campgrounds just outside of town, but worry nagged at him and he thought it best to stick around in case Pressley called. So, Hayden worked in his backyard, piling up freshly cut wood into a neat stack beside the small shed, then he raked up the dead grass and leaves. Finally, he cut the lawn even though it didn't really need it.

Bone-tired and sweaty, Hayden showered and changed into a pair of sweat pants and a T-shirt. He lay down on the couch and flicked on the television. His townhouse, though modest, was rustic and quaint — just what Shaun loved. He was surrounded by her good taste and it was a comfort to him. She'd decorated their home meticulously, doing each room until she felt it was perfect. But, the lack of Shaun, her complete and total absence, baffled him. He spoke to her all the time, sometimes even getting down on his knees and asking God to send him a sign from her. Something to let him know she was still around.

And at times, he got mad at God. Why did he take Shaun away so soon? They were to be married. He'd thought about the children they might have had. A daughter with Shaun's blonde hair and big green eyes, and maybe a son with a splatter of freckles across his nose.

Those thoughts of what might have been sometimes morphed into an aching need to switch them off. He thought of the beer in the fridge: something to take off the edge. TV was useless, filled with reality shows and dumb-ass sitcoms. After Shaun's death, he drank a lot, and not just beer. He'd hung out at the Main Street pub, alone, preferring it that way. Shutting the door on his old life. His friends didn't know what to say or how to help. Hell, nothing could help him, and everyone knew it, including his sister and parents. He had to hit rock bottom to find his way back to the world of the living.

His mind turned to Pressley and surprisingly, his urge to drink evaporated. Why was he was so taken with her? She looked nothing like Shaun, but there was *something* that reminded him of her. Maybe it was her passion for animals? Or that she left a lucrative job to do something her heart desired and to make a difference in the world? That must be it — Shaun came from a wealthy family and could have lived a life of leisure, but she chose not to. She was not the "born on third base, thinking she'd hit a home run" kind of woman, and neither was Pressley.

He smiled when he thought of the sweet, awkward girl Pressley turned into every time he saw her, and how she blurted out whatever she was thinking. She had no filter and he loved that. Yet, despite her non-existent internal editor, Pressley still managed to remain a puzzle — made up of one-part librarian and one-part nutty professor, but with a hearty sprinkling of sexy.

Hayden plucked up his cell phone from the coffee table. Should he call to see how she was getting along with Jasper, or wait to see if she called him? He let out a huge sigh and threw caution to the wind.

* * * * *

Jasper woke from his nap a bit groggy, but eager to sniff out his new surroundings. Pressley sat beside him, leaning against the wall of the family room while he snoozed in his bed. She, too, had nodded off a few times only to jerk awake whenever the dog moved or made a noise in his sleep. She kept his collar and leash on him and tied the other end to a leg of the couch. She'd also put out a sedative-filled treat on the kitchen counter along with the muzzle, just in case.

    Being completely alone with the dog was not really scary — she didn't think he'd bite her; the dog had been nothing but affectionate with her — but it did feel strange, and she was the cautious type. Maybe it was because she hadn't lived with anyone, not even a pet, for a very long time. She'd learned to be self-sufficient since her mother's death.

Her phone buzzed and although she was tempted to answer, she ignored it. Right now, she had bigger things to attend to. She watched as the dog slowly and carefully stepped out of his bed, nose to the floor taking in the new scents around him. After circling the room, he raised a leg and peed on the wall.

"Jasper, no!" Her voice pitched higher than she'd intended.

Pressley grabbed him by the collar, unclipped his leash and led him to the patio door. She breathed a sigh of relief when he trotted along willingly, even looking up at her, approval shining in his eyes. How could she stay mad at him? The thought that he wasn't housebroken hadn't even occurred to her until now.

When she opened the door, the dog froze, and sniffed the fresh air. His hackles bristled. She slid open the screen and took a step backwards. Jasper walked out into the yard. His nose once again turned to the ground as he sniffed his way around shrubs, trees, and the open grassy area. Pressley's yard was large enough for a dog like Jasper to run around in, and it was fully fenced.

After peeing on everything he sniffed, he plopped to the ground and wriggled on his back in a patch of mud.

"NO! Stop it!" Forgetting herself, Pressley made her way to the mud-covered dog and took him by the collar. This time he snapped at her — teeth just catching the thin flesh of her wrist, but not drawing blood.

Pressley was more astonished than afraid and as soon as she realized the dog had bitten her, Jasper had fled. She watched amazed and shocked as the dog leapt over the back fence of her yard in a single bound.

~ Twelve ~

When she didn't answer her phone, or reply to his texts, Hayden hightailed it to the shelter. Janet had already left for the day. Nevertheless, he'd gone to the shelter to try to find out where Pressley lived. He pulled open desk drawers, only to discover copious amounts of paper in Janet's, and nothing except a green felt marker and paper clips in Pressley's.

Next, he riffled through the files in the cabinet in the corner of the office. Maybe the legal paperwork Pressley had filled out that morning for the Westons would be in there. Again, he found nothing.

A strange noise at the front door caught his attention — it wasn't a knock but a rattle as if someone was shaking the glass pane. He walked over to check it out. He could hardly believe it. Jasper was on the other side of the glass door, pawing to be let in.

There were patches of mud on his back and around his face. Hayden opened the door slowly, so he wouldn't scare him off, and moved out of his way as Jasper walked through the door. The dog shook with hearty abandon, speckling the walls and Hayden with dirt. Hayden rolled his eyes. "Did you have to do that?" Jasper growled and sidestepped away from him.

Hayden peeked outside for Pressley. Could she be bringing him back? But she was nowhere to be seen, and the only vehicles in the parking lot were his and Jose's: one of the volunteers. How on earth had the dog gotten so dirty? The poor thing looked as if he'd just pulled himself out of a pit of quicksand.

Hayden closed the door and turned to find Jasper at the end of the hall, nose pressed against the door that led to the kennels. "You wanna go home? Poor guy, you've been here so long you figure you belong at the shelter, don't you, boy?" He took Jasper by the collar and with the other hand, opened the door to lead him through. There was always the chance one of the animals was out of its cage for a little exercise and a change of scenery, and there would be no telling what Jasper would do if he spotted another animal.

When the coast was clear, Hayden tugged on Jasper's collar. With a snarl, the dog turned and sunk his teeth into Hayden's forearm. "Shit!" he yelled, pulling away.

Jasper's growl sunk an octave as he moved toward Hayden, head low, eyes trained on him. Hayden was now pinned against the steel door with no chance of escape. He thought about jumping back through to the other side of the threshold and slamming the door on the dog, but there was no way he could be quick enough; Jasper was just too close.

His mind switched gears quickly as panic-laced adrenaline urged him on. He tried another tack. "Okay, buddy. It's okay. You wanna cookie?" His tone was high-pitched and friendly. The dog's ears pricked up, and his head tilted at the mention of "cookie" but he didn't look any friendlier. Hayden glanced at his arm. It felt as if it was on fire. Blood ran in rivulets and dripped off his fingertips, polka-dotting the floor. He was certain a trip to the hospital was in his future — that is if he had a future. Right now, he had to find a way to corral Jasper into a cage and quick, but the dog kept him pinned to the wall with just a sidelong stare.

A sudden shuffle of footsteps filled Hayden with hope — someone was coming! He moved out from his spot behind the door and Jasper's jaws clamped down again, this time taking hold of his calf. The animal shook with all its might, its powerful neck and head helping to tear through Hayden's jeans and into the flesh beneath. He kicked at the dog with his good leg, but lost his balance and crashed to the floor. Jasper was on him now: the animal's large blocky body pinned Hayden in place. A tidal wave of fear had the blood pulsing in Hayden's ears. Then he felt the dog's nose, cold and wet against his throat. He turned away as best he could and threw a hand up for cover. This was it, he thought. The dog was going to kill him.

As if by magic, the animal was suddenly moved up and away from him and he heard Jasper's whimpering cries echoing in the cement-walled building. Hayden looked up to see one of the volunteers on the other end of a restraining pole, the metal loop around the struggling dog's neck.

"Got 'im," Jose said as he wrangled Jasper away. "Be right back, man. Hang on. You're gonna be okay."

~ Thirteen ~

The painkillers were just kicking in when Hayden's cell phone rang. Jose had been kind enough to not only rescue him, but also drive him to the emergency room of Quick Rivers General where his arm was stitched up, and his leg bandaged. Now, he lay in his bed at home propped up against a few pillows. Jose had offered to stay to keep him company, but he thanked him profusely and told him he needed to be alone. The meds were fogging up his mind and he was too worried about Pressley and Jasper to be good company.

He browsed Netflix on his laptop for something to take his mind off the pain and the fact he'd eventually have to deliver terrible news to deliver to Pressley, if only he could get a hold of her. Before he left, Jose suggested they call Janet to let her know what happened and for a moment, Hayden considered this — maybe he could get Pressley's address from her. He wanted to make sure she was okay and prayed to God that the dog had just run away and not attacked her. He'd also considered calling the police, not because the dog attacked him, but to have them check up on Pressley. But his instincts told him not to tell Janet or call the cops — at least not yet. That would ring the alarm and put Jasper back on the path to certain death. Jasper was safely in his cage at the Paws and Claws shelter, at least for the time being.

Despite the wave of relaxation that began to flow through him courtesy of the painkillers, his heart leapt when he saw Pressley's name light up his phone.

"Hello?" he said quickly.

"Jasper's gone! I've looked all over and can't find him. I've been walking the streets, looking for him for hours. Should I call the police, or put up posters, or—"

"He's safe. He came back to the shelter and he's in his cage. Pretty smart, I guess. It's the only real home he's known."

He heard a whoosh of relief from the other end of the phone and Hayden wished he could share in that feeling. He rubbed tired eyes with his good hand and said, "Pressley, there's something I have to tell you." Without waiting for a response, he continued before his courage deserted him. "First, I need to know you're okay. The dog didn't bite you, did he?"

She hesitated, then said, "No, I'm fine."

At least he could be grateful for that. He soldiered on, "Jasper attacked me today at the shelter. I saw him at the door and let him in, then he turned on me. I've got ten stitches in my forearm and a couple of puncture wounds on my leg. Thank God Jose was there to help me. He got Jasper off me before he could do any more damage."

Silence. A seemingly never-ending silence, and then: "I'm so sorry," followed by sniffles and sobs. "Can I come over?"

Hayden was exhausted, but he'd never tell Pressley not to come over. He gave her his address and waited, trying not to nod off.

* * * * *

A knock at the door startled Hayden awake. He'd fallen asleep after all and it took a moment before he remembered what had happened and that it must be Pressley at the door. He made his way from the bedroom to let her in, giving his head a good shake to clear the cobwebs before swinging the door open.

Her eyes widened, and her hand flew to her mouth when she saw the bandages. "Oh my God," she whispered.

"It's not as bad as it looks." He smiled. "I've been through worse. Come on in." He tried to take her jacket to hang it in the closet, but she insisted on doing it herself.

"Coffee? Tea?" Hayden asked as he walked to the kitchen with Pressley on his heels.

He pulled out a chair for her. "Sit."

She took a seat and answered his questions with a quick shake of her head. "Do *you* want something? Have you eaten?"

Hayden sat opposite her. "I'm good. I had a sandwich with my painkillers." He picked up the prescription bottle sitting on the kitchen table and gave it a shake. "Take with food."

He was wearing gray track pants with holes in the knees and a faded black T-shirt and he knew he looked as if he'd been sleeping. "Am I disturbing you? Maybe you need some rest?"

"No! I'm happy you're here."

"I never could have imagined this would happen. All I did was let him out into the yard.

He'd been sleeping a long time and when he woke up, I figured he'd have to pee. He was fine with me. Didn't give me the slightest sense that I should be wary of him, but as soon as he was outside, after sniffing around a bit, he took off running to the end of the yard and jumped over the fence! It didn't cross my mind that he'd do that. I should have called you sooner, but I was frantic, looking for him everywhere." A smile curled her lips. "At least he's safe now. When I get him home, I'll only take him out on a leash and keep him crated. It makes sense since he's used to his crate at the shelter. Of course, I'll make it homier, more comfortable. I'll put in a bunch of toys and—"

Hayden put a hand on hers. "You can't take him home, Pressley."

Her eyes grew to the size of silver dollars. "What? Why not?"

"He's a dangerous animal. He's unadoptable." Hayden felt the burn of tears and blinked them away. He wanted more than anything to kiss the beautiful woman in front of him. The woman whose heart he'd just ripped out. But he wouldn't dare. He continued, "Jasper should never have gone home with you. Everything's my fault." He held his arm up. "Even this. If I hadn't pushed so hard to find that dog a home, he would never have jumped your fence, and he never would have bitten me. I'm sorry."

She stood up, a complex look of confusion, sadness, and anger played on her face. "You don't have to apologize for anything, Hayden. I'm really, really sorry about what Jasper did to you. I feel terrible about it, really, I do, but as soon as Monday morning comes, I'm going to the shelter to pick up my dog and bring him home with me."

"You can't. Maybe I'm not being clear enough, Pressley. Jasper is a *dangerous* animal. There's no way to save him now. He's going to be put down Monday morning." He'd kept the incident from Janet for the time being, but he'd be calling Dr. Graham as soon as Pressley left. How could he let her take a dog as large and powerful as Jasper back into her home after he'd experienced firsthand what the animal was capable of?

Her jaw dropped, and tears sprang to her eyes. "What? No!"

He stood beside her and put his good arm around her. "It has to be done."

She leaned her head on his shoulder and tears ran down her face, "Did you call the police? Did you file a complaint?"

"No, but Jose was a witness. It's just a matter of time."

He felt her deflate. Her shoulders sank, and his T-shirt was wet with tears. She wrapped her arms around his neck and sobbed.

"What a mess I've made. I've barely set foot into Paws and Claws and look at the disaster I've created."

Hayden pulled away to look into her eyes. "Don't say that. You may not have saved Jasper, but you saved me. Please, for your sake, let the dog go." He kissed her forehead.

"I can't work at the shelter anymore."

Hayden's heart felt as if it was about to stop. "You've only just started. Janet can't do what you do. She's more of a fixture at the place and does little more than shuffle papers. We need you." He hesitated then added, "I need you."

She didn't answer, only made her way to the door and opened it. The cool, late fall air sent a chill through him.

"I still want my dog," Pressley said through her tears.

But did she want him? he wondered.

~ Fourteen ~

Pressley wouldn't let her mind wander to what Hayden said was inevitable. Jasper was hers and he was coming back home on Monday, and that was that. She'd bought a twenty-foot lead she could clip to his collar to keep him from jumping the fence.

Pressley contemplated calling her friend, Emma, but they'd grown apart since Emma found herself a boyfriend and was spending every second with him. She'd never felt lonelier. She needed to talk to someone about her problems with the dog and ask for their thoughts. It was a good idea to keep him, wasn't it? It was the right thing to do? She wished she could talk to her parents, too. Her mom always knew what to say to comfort her. Dad was, well, not quite there anymore, and despite his fairly young age of just sixty, he lived in an assisted-living home. Her mom, Joanie, had died of cancer three years ago — shortly after, Pressley started therapy. But she was feeling stronger now. Her therapist had taught her how to manage her anxiety as well as ways to boost her self-esteem.

She wondered if others saw her as a shy, introvert. Or, did they see a perfectionistic snob? Pressley thought about that for a while and decided she was a bit of both. True, she was quiet but when she clicked with someone, she was a motor-mouth. She liked to think of herself as discerning — only giving her time to those who really mattered. Why waste it on chitchat? She preferred a small group of close friends to large parties. Did that make her an introvert? Maybe, but what was wrong with that?

She poured a glass of wine and settled onto the sofa. Pressley eyed her phone. She had to admit she was watching for texts from Hayden and wondered if he'd told Janet she planned to quit. She wondered too if she would really go through with it. Despite only just starting, she liked her job. It was low stress, with little responsibility, and most of all, she loved the animals. It was what she needed.

* * * * *

Monday came quickly and Pressley — who'd spent the night before tossing and turning, waiting for morning — was in the parking lot of Paws and Claws before the sun rose, waiting for someone to arrive and hoping it would be Janet and not Hayden or Dr. Graham. Well, maybe seeing Hayden wouldn't be so bad.

She had the keys to the place but since the idea of quitting was front and center, she didn't feel right about going inside when no one else was there.

Another hour passed before Janet's white Honda Civic pulled up beside her Prius. Janet looked over and gave her a little wave. Pressley guessed Hayden hadn't talked to Janet after all.

"Good morning! Got here at the same time, did we?" Janet asked as she exited her car.

Pressley took stock of the woman — bright smile, extra-large coffee in hand, hair done, face made up — nothing to signify anything was out of sorts. "You speak to Hayden over the weekend?" Pressley asked.

"No, hon. Why? Something wrong? How's Jasper? You have a good few days with him?"

Pressley picked up her pace as she walked the short distance to the front door. She unlocked it and held the door open for Janet. Once inside, she answered Janet's questions.

"Jasper's here. He jumped the fence in my yard and came back to the shelter. Since it's been his home for so long, I suppose it was just instinct." She took measure of her boss.

Janet's jaw fell slack, but shock was quickly replaced with curiosity. "How'd you know all this?"

"Hayden was here when he came back, and he let him in but — and this isn't good news — Jasper bit him. Got hold of his forearm and leg. Jose got the dog off him and took Hayden to the hospital. He had to have stitches." She was on a roll, no use stopping now. "I'm pretty sure Dr. Graham is coming in this morning. Hayden says he's a lost cause and has to be put down, but I'm here to collect him before that happens. He's my dog and I've legally adopted him. As far as I know, no one's called the police or made a report. I don't know what Hayden told the doctors at the hospital, but I imagine if he told the truth, the cops would have paid me a visit as Jasper's owner and since that hasn't happened, I figure no one said a thing." This time she didn't stay to assess Janet's reaction. She made her way down the hall and called over her shoulder, "Maybe I shouldn't work here anymore either."

"No!" Janet beat Pressley to the door and plastered herself against it, arms outstretched to prevent her entrance. Janet was splayed against the door like a giant starfish.

"Please, Janet. This is ridiculous. I'm within my rights. Would you please move out of the way?"

Janet looked past her, and then a masculine voice spoke. "Move aside, Janet. Pressley, I'm sure you're not going to want to witness what has to be done."

It was Dr. Graham, tall and distinguished, looking more like a corporate lawyer than a vet, with his neatly styled salt and pepper hair. He wore a suit and tie, not a white smock. But he was holding a leather case that reminded Pressley of an old-fashioned doctor's bag.

"Who called you? Was it Hayden?" Pressley asked.

"Does that really matter?" he replied.

Janet moved out of the way, but Pressley took up the space she'd vacated. "Yes, it does."

Dr. Graham sighed his frustration. "No. Jose called and told me what happened."

"The dog is legally mine. You don't have my permission to put him down," Pressley said, injecting confidence into her tone and hoping neither Janet nor Dr. Graham heard the hitch in her voice.

"I can call the police, if that's what it'll take," he said and reached past her for the doorknob. "It's my professional opinion that the dog cannot be rehabilitated. He must be put down to keep people safe, and that includes you!"

He pulled open the door and made his way into the kennel area, the steel door slamming in his wake.

Pressley reached to open the door, but Janet put a hand on hers before she could. "Don't, hon. Please, just go on home. Take the day off. Take a couple if you like but come back to work when you're feeling better. This place needs you. You're doing a fabulous job and there will always be another dog to adopt. Let's face it, Jasper just wasn't the one for you. Hell's bells, I don't think anyone could tame that wild thing." She shook her head in a show of sympathy. "He did love you in his own way though, so don't forget that, honey. You were the only one he'd even let near, but he's a danger to others and if you take him out of here, only God knows what else he'll do."

An ache as real as if she'd been punched in the gut almost floored her, but Pressley held tight. She knew it now — there was no hope for Jasper. Even if she did push past Janet, Dr. Graham was probably already prepping to do his job. Poor Jasper, poor soul, he wasn't given a fighting chance in this life and that was so unfair. Someone hurt him, broke his soul, and turned him vicious. She knew how that could happen. Her life wasn't ideal either — the pain of what happened to her parents had pushed her farther into herself and kept her there. But she was a human being, and no one was going to kill her just because she had issues, so why should that happen to Jasper?

The fight had drained from her. She turned to Janet and said, "I don't think I can come back. I didn't realize how hard it would be to not be able to save all the animals. I wanted to work here because it was a no-kill shelter, and that's not what it will be when Jasper is put to death."

"Oh, hon," Janet said, "please, give it some thought. Don't be hasty."

But her words fell on deaf ears as Pressley turned and walked away.

~ Fifteen ~

Hayden came through the back door. He hoped to God he wouldn't run into Dr. Graham, but his prayers weren't answered. He spotted the vet at Jasper's cage, his medical bag opened. Was he too late?

He'd spent the night hatching a plan; as ludicrous and dangerous as it was, it was the only thing he could think to do. He'd arranged a jailbreak of sorts and was equipped with a muzzle and leash. If he could get the dog back to his house, maybe, just maybe he'd be able to earn Jasper's trust and make him into a real pet. He was risking further injury and, just the day before, was convinced the dog was a lost cause, but if he wanted Pressley he realized, he'd have to fight for Jasper.

He picked up his pace and called, "Dr. Graham! Hold up."

The vet was crouched beside the cage and looked up as Hayden approached. "Don't bother trying to talk me out of this, Hayden." He was holding a syringe in one gloved hand.

"The Westons said to wait," he lied.

Dr. Graham rose to his feet. "What? You've got to be kidding."

"Not at all. I called them and said there was a mistake, that I'd been bitten by a new intake and not Jasper."

The vet smirked. "Jose told me what happened. This dog's had too many reprieves already."

Hayden moved closer. Jasper was lying on his side, asleep. "No! You didn't—"

"Relax, he's just sedated." He pointed to Hayden's arm. "Don't want that to happen to me, too."

"So, he's okay?"

"For now."

Hayden's face was a thundercloud. "Leave the dog alone." He put a hand on the top of the cage preventing the doctor from opening it further. "You should go now."

Indignation was written all over the older man's face. He clearly was not used to being told what to do.

"Hayden, be reasonable. All of this back and forth is ridiculous. I was happy when I thought we'd found Jasper a home, I really was, but you know as well as I do that there will be a next time. And the next time that dog bites someone, it just might be Pressley." He tapped his temple. "Use your head."

"I've already thought this through, Doc, and believe me, the back and forth has driven me nuts, but if things don't work out this time, I'll take care of Jasper myself."

"You serious?"

"As a heart attack."

The vet threw up his hands in surrender. "I'll leave him be for another day or two, but I don't see a way out of this for that dog."

* * * * *

Hayden wondered if he should speak to Janet before taking the dog with him. He'd tell her his plan. She'd agree it was the right thing to do, wouldn't she? But then again, with all the back and forth, the drama, the moral dilemmas, he couldn't be sure what she'd say. What if she wanted to consult the Westons? Then he was screwed — if word got back to them that Jasper had attacked him, that would be the end of the road.

"To hell with it," he said aloud. "Better to do what you want and apologize later than to ask for permission and be denied."

He opened the cage door, picked up the dog and took him out to his truck, placing the groggy dog on the back seat.

He ran back into the shelter and grabbed an old kennel. The extras were folded up and stored against the wall near the supply room. He couldn't be sure he was alone in the back, but he hadn't seen any of the volunteers yet, so he carefully and quietly took the first in the pile, closed the back door and locked it. Then he put the kennel into the bed of his truck.

* * * * *

Taking the dog to his house was probably not his best option. Dr. Graham would more than likely tip off Janet about what just happened. Janet might be foolish enough to call the Westons or, God forbid, the police.

Two hours later, when he pulled into the driveway in front of Shaun's cottage, he could hear Jasper beginning to stir. The cottage held a special place in his heart. It was where he and Shaun went almost every weekend, a private sanctuary that the family had given Shaun after she'd graduated from college. Hayden hadn't been here since her death and he was pretty sure he was trespassing. The cottage was now either in her parents' name, or sold. Either way, it looked empty and it was the only hideout he had.

Before he left for the cottage, he'd picked up supplies, including dog food, treats, and toys, as well as stopping by his house to grab his laptop and a few things for himself to munch on. He remembered there being Wi-Fi at the cottage when he and Shaun spent time there, but there was no way to know if it had been turned off. People like the Westons, with money to burn, tended to forget about little things like that. At least he hoped so.

Before getting out of the truck, he muzzled Jasper — the dog was still sleepy enough to be docile, then he left for a moment to snoop around the cottage. There were no cars in the driveway, a great sign, and after looking in the large front windows to make sure no one was there, his heart leapt when he saw that it looked exactly the same as it did when he and Shaun used to stay there. He tried the front door, but of course it was locked. He pulled on the windows — again locked. Then it struck him. He still had a key! He ran to his truck, grabbed his keys and was back at the front door in a couple of seconds. If his luck held up, the locks would still be the same. His hands shook as he tried the key — it slid in and, with a turn, he heard the deadbolt click open.

* * * * *

By the time he'd set up the kennel and brought in the supplies, Jasper was awake and watching him through the window in the back seat of the truck. It was time to bring him into the cottage. Hayden opened the truck door just a crack. Jasper was there in a nanosecond, his large nose pressed against the opening. He sniffed and grunted and rubbed his muzzled face against the seat, trying to get the muzzle off.

Hayden waited for the right moment and when the dog turned, he clipped the leash onto his collar. Jasper bucked like a bull, pulling the leash taut. Hayden gave him a little slack and let him continue his rebellion. Jasper jumped onto the floor of the truck and charged at Hayden who was standing on the other side of the open door, but Hayden moved out of the way and Jasper landed on the gravel driveway, somersaulting his way to a stop. "Well, at least you're out of the truck," Hayden said as he closed the door.

Getting the dog indoors wasn't as hard as Hayden had anticipated. In fact, Jasper led the way. His nose to the ground, he sniffed his way up the stairs, onto the porch and through the open door of the cottage.

As soon as Jasper spotted the kennel, he made his way inside it just as Hayden expected. The kennel meant safety to Jasper — his instincts had kicked in. Hayden unclipped the leash through the bars and then did his best to undo the muzzle without getting bitten. The dog growled but let him do it. It was almost as if he realized what Hayden was trying to do and ridding himself of the uncomfortable thing wrapped around his head was welcomed.

In the cage was a bowl of food and water as well as an old blanket, which would have to serve as a makeshift bed. Jasper didn't seem to mind — he turned in a circle and settled onto the blanket.

Hayden set his laptop on the kitchen table, a few feet away from the dog, and powered it up. He waited and once again prayed. Finally, a dialogue box popped up asking for a password. "Yes," he whispered in triumph. There was indeed Wi-Fi. He typed in what he thought was the password and got an error message. "Damn it!" His luck was bound to run out at some point. He racked his brain trying to remember as many of Shaun's passwords as he could, but time and again, they failed. He took a few deep, calming breaths. He'd figure this out if it killed him. He got up and pulled open drawers and cupboards looking for a notebook, or a scrap of paper — anything where a password could have been written down. Nothing!

His cell phone rang, startling him. He saw that it was Janet and turned it off. He didn't know how much time he had before someone figured out where he was. He needed to get on the Internet as soon as possible. He turned his eyes skyward and spoke. "Shaun, if you can hear me, I need your help. Please, help me figure this out." It was stupid, of course. His dead girlfriend wasn't about to whisper the password in his ear. Or was she? The words came out of the blue —

ShaunlovesHayden22. He typed them in and got a signal.

The subconscious mind remembers everything, he told himself. He just needed to clear his head and let the long-forgotten password make its way to the surface.

* * * * *

The signal wasn't strong, and the Internet was slow, but it was good enough. For the next three hours, he read everything he could find online about training the untrainable and helping the "unhelpable" until finally, he was ready to confront his attacker. Anxiety still niggled at him and he tried to push the fear away.

When he turned his attention to Jasper, the dog's low growls echoed through the small space. The dog lunged, snapping his powerful jaws and sending Hayden back a step.

"Whoa there, Jasper," he said softly. "Be a good boy. I'm not going to hurt you. Besides, you're the one with the big, sharp teeth, remember?" He lifted his injured arm to show the dog. Jasper growled his response.

Hayden felt sorry for the animal. How many times had he escaped death? "And I thought only cats had nine lives."

He remembered how close the dog had come to being put down earlier that day. Dr. Graham had already given the dog a sedative. Next, he would have opened the door and injected Jasper with a dose of pentobarbital. The dog's heart and brain functions would have shut down within a minute or two, and then he'd be gone. His body would be burned, and it would be as if he'd never existed.

Shaun had been cremated. Was that how it was for her now? Like she'd never existed? Of course not, he thought. Shaun was loved, and she did many good things. She would be remembered, always. He wanted

Jasper to have another chance. There had to be good in him somewhere. Dogs weren't born bad, they were turned — made bad by abusive owners.

Hayden looked at the scarred patches of skin on the dog, patches where fur no longer grew. There was a tear in his left ear, probably from a one of his many fights. He wanted to pet the dog, to tell him he didn't have to be mean anymore and that if he would only behave, he'd have a good life with Pressley.

"I'm going to sit down now," he said and then sat on the floor in front of the cage. Jasper snarled and stared back narrow-eyed, looking as if he wanted nothing more than to tear Hayden apart.

Hayden didn't move from his spot in front of the cage for almost an hour, letting Jasper bark and growl, until finally, the dog grew tired and stopped his protests.

He was also careful not to make direct eye contact. He stole glances and spoke softly. Another half an hour passed until Jasper finally sat; soon after, he lay down, still facing Hayden, nose twitching.

Moving slowly, Hayden reached into his knapsack where he'd stored the dog treats. They were the crème de la crème — not just the run-of-the mill treats from the shelter. He had dried beef jerky, dried liver, chicken jerky, pigs' ears, and minced chicken. With his good hand, he teased out a couple pieces of dried liver. Jasper sat up, and this time, he didn't growl.

Hayden put the treat in front of the dog's cage, so he could sniff it. Jasper looked from the treat to Hayden and then pressed his nose against the bars.

Hayden moved the pieces of dried liver closer so that they were touching the bars. Jasper's tongue flicked at them, moving them away and out of his reach. The dog whined and pawed at the bars. "Easy, easy. I'll get them for you," Hayden whispered. This time he dropped them inside the cage. Jasper snapped them up and stared at Hayden expectantly.

"Looks like you enjoyed that. You want more?" He took a different treat, a piece of chicken jerky, from his bag. Jasper salivated at the sight of it.

With a deep breath to summon up courage, Hayden handed the jerky to the dog. Jasper drew back, then clapped one big paw down on it and pulled it to him. He growled a warning, as if to say, "Back off! This is mine."

For hours, Hayden fed the dog small treats until he finally gained confidence that Jasper wasn't going to chomp off one of his fingers. Eventually, he was feeding him from two fingers he'd inserted through the bars.

Hayden could see the sun beginning to set outside the large picture windows. An orangey-red glow filled the dimly lit room. The day had passed quickly, and Hayden wondered how many people knew about Jasper's jailbreak by now. Janet must have known — why else all the phone calls? Did Pressley know?

He stretched and yawned as he rose. He needed a break and searched the kitchen cabinets for a kettle. He found an old battered aluminum one under the sink, rinsed it with tap water then poured a bottle of water into it and set it on a burner to boil. He'd brought instant coffee, a package of social tea cookies, a few granola bars, and a Thermos with him and not much else. While he waited for the water to boil, he turned on his phone. The screen told him he'd missed fifteen calls, all from Janet. He turned it off again not bothering to listen to the voice mails.

He drank his coffee in front of the kennel, feeding the dog and speaking to him. He told him stories about his childhood, using a soothing tone. It didn't matter what he said, he knew, just as long as he didn't sound threatening. Jasper stayed quiet, no growling for the time being, and when Hayden finished his coffee, he slowly got to his feet.

Jasper moved to the back of the cage, his eyes trained on Hayden's every move. "Okay, buddy, it's time for the real test. I'm opening the door now, Jasper. Please be a good boy." He unlatched the door, swung it open, and stepped backwards until he was several feet away. Hayden held on to his knapsack of treats, but decided to kneel. He'd appear less threating than if he was standing.

Jasper took his time in exiting the kennel — with one step forward, he'd pause, sniff the air, wait for what felt like an eternity to Hayden then finally take another step until he was all the way out of the kennel.

Hayden cooed, "Good boy. You want another treat?" He kept an eye on the dog as he dug into his cache and, this time, he brought out the most coveted treat: minced chicken. He had no dish, so he emptied the plastic baggie onto the floor by his feet. Jasper moved quicker this time, making his way over to Hayden, the scent of the raw chicken an irresistible draw.

Hayden squirted a dollop of antibacterial lotion from the bottle hanging off the outside of his bag, hoping it would remove the lingering scent of chicken. Jasper looked up to see what was going on. Hayden tensed, readying for an attack that didn't come. Instead, the dog nosed his knapsack, searching for more chicken.

"Can't believe you're not full yet," Hayden said and absently reached down to pet the dog. He didn't realize his indiscretion until his hand was on Jasper's head. The dog's ears pricked up, but he let Hayden pet him. He even looked as if he was enjoying the attention. Hayden scratched behind the dog's ears and then under his collar. Jasper turned his head this way and that to allow Hayden access to those hard to get to places, but soon slunk back to the safety of his kennel. Hayden didn't close the door. Jasper curled into a ball on his blanket, facing Hayden.

Feeding the dog was a big step. Hopefully, Jasper would trust him even if just a little because he was the dog's only source of food. At the shelter, he had lots of people around who'd fill his bowl with kibble. Most made a hurried job of it because of Jasper's fearsome reputation and so the dog had never bonded with anyone over food.

He was also buoyed by Jasper allowing Hayden to pet him. There were no aggressive moves, no growls, no narrow-eyed sidelong glances — all great signs. Yet, he knew there was still a lot of work ahead if he was to fully win over Jasper. And, the dog not only had to trust Hayden, but Hayden had to trust the dog, too.

When Hayden walked around to the other side of the cage, Jasper turned so he was still facing him. But soon, he slept, content and finally comfortable enough in Hayden's presence to close his eyes. Hayden, for his part, was quiet as he scrolled through a few more articles about dog training. But after a while, the growling in his stomach was more than he could bear and the thought of quelling it with more coffee wasn't good enough. He got up to grab a snack from his knapsack. Jasper's eyes popped open and he jumped to his feet. His hackles rose, freezing Hayden to the spot. He dared not move, not yet — not until the dog settled. Minutes passed like hours until, finally, Jasper sat and no longer looked like he was going to eat Hayden for dinner.

    Hayden reached into his bag and instead of pulling out one of the handful of granola bars he'd thrown in, his hand found a tennis ball. His hunger would have to wait as an idea formed in his mind. He bounced the ball as he walked to Jasper's kennel.

"You wanna play?" He showed the ball to the dog. Hayden knew the dog hadn't had much playtime in his short life.

Jasper tilted his head, as if trying to understand the question.

He bounced the ball again. This time, Jasper got to his feet and took a step forward. Hayden's heart beat hard against his rib cage. The dog seemed to want to play, but how could he be sure? He knelt and tossed the ball into the air, just high enough for Jasper to easily make the catch. The dog chomped down on it with powerful jaws and then walked over to Hayden and deposited it at his feet, putting a relieved smile on Hayden's face.

"You like this, don't you, boy?" Hayden took in his surroundings. The cottage was small with an open-concept living and kitchen area. There was nowhere to throw the ball to make it a real game of fetch.

The dog yipped, and his tail motored back and forth, his eyes trained on the ball in

Hayden's hand. A good game of catch would do wonders, Hayden thought. It would not only tire Jasper but also bond them further.

Hayden rolled the ball to the dog. Jasper scooped it up gladly. The distraction gave Hayden time to clip on the long lead he'd brought with him for trips outdoors. When Jasper realized he was tethered, he dropped the ball and strained against the lead.

"It's okay, buddy. Let's go outside. You probably have to do your business anyway." Hayden picked up the ball and gave Jasper some slack as he headed toward the door. He flicked on the outside lights. It was dark, but the lights were bright enough to illuminate the front yard. Surprisingly, the dog followed and soon, they were outside. In the distance, Hayden caught a glimpse of the lake. Memories flooded back — so many summers were spent on that dock with Shaun, so many dips in the lake and then lying in the sun to dry off. They'd enjoyed a beer or two in the

Muskoka chairs he'd built for them. He remembered that too and the lovemaking. Somehow, it was sweeter in the summer when all cares seemed to fade away.

A tug on the lead pulled him from his thoughts. Jasper was sniffing for a place to do his business and once he was done, he trotted back to Hayden and planted himself at his feet. Hayden threw the ball in the air and caught it — he had the dog's attention. Jasper's head followed the tennis ball into its launch and back down to Hayden's hand. He barked excitedly and jumped up on Hayden, sending him back a step.

"Looks like I found your weak spot," Hayden said with a smile. He threw the ball fifteen feet or so, just far enough for the dog to be able to get to it while still on his tether.

Jasper was back in a flash. He was a natural. Some dogs didn't bother to come back with the ball, not wanting to give it up once they'd retrieved it, but Jasper was smart enough to realize that the game would go on if he gave the ball back to Hayden.

"Good boy!" He tried to pet the dog, but Jasper wanted to play and moved out of reach. "Okay, we'll just play, then." Again and again, Hayden threw the ball. Again and again, Jasper brought it back.

Hayden had a thought. Though he'd be taking a risk, he thought the odds were in his favor. He unclipped the lead and launched the ball as far as he could across the yard and onto the gravel driveway. He saw its orange neon glow as it bounced and finally came to a stop on the other side of the driveway. Jasper saw it too. He was off in a flash.

Hayden said a silent prayer that the dog would return. What if Jasper, sensing his freedom, just kept on going? The sound of his own heart pounding grew loud in his ears and it was only when he saw the dog running back with the ball in his mouth that he began to relax.

They played a while longer until Jasper, with tongue lolling, looked as if he was about to drop. "Better get back inside, buddy. Looks like you need some water," he told the panting dog. But when he picked up the ball, Jasper gave a high-pitched bark, urging Hayden to throw it again.

"Okay." He laughed. "But this is it. One last time."

His last launch was the farthest yet. The dog took off after it, his eyes trained on the ball, but when it touched down, it hit rock and bounced down the hill toward the lake. Hayden walked as quickly as possible — running was difficult with his sore leg — to the top of the hill. He hoped Jasper would still be able to find the ball in the dark. The porch lights didn't reach past the crest of the hill. Thankfully, the moon was full, and the sky dotted with stars, so Hayden easily spotted Jasper. His heart took off in a sprint when he saw the dog running onto the dock. And then, he heard the distant sound of water splashing as Jasper ran out of dock and fell into the lake.

Hayden took off down the hill, his calf muscles aching as the strain pulled at his torn flesh. The night was chilly, and the water would be freezing. He had to get to Jasper as quickly as possible. He could hear the dog splashing, but saw nothing in the darkness. He knelt on the dock and pulled his phone from his back pocket, activating the flashlight. He spotted him, flailing, confused, not knowing which way to swim to shore. Did he need to jump into the lake to save the dog, or would the light be enough to help Jasper find his way out of trouble?

"Ah, hell," he said as he laid his phone on the dock and jumped in. The stabbing cold of the water stole his breath, but he was able to grab he dog, wrapping an arm under one of Jasper's legs and around his chest as he swam to shore with only the moonlight to show the way.

The dog was heavy, at least eighty pounds, Hayden figured, yet despite his stitched-up forearm and aching leg, he managed to carry him back up the hill to the warmth and safety of the cottage.

~ Sixteen ~

Pressley could think of no other place to go. So, here she was in the antiseptic room where her father lived, at the Patrick M. Mitchell Long-Term Health Facility. It was a twenty-minute drive from her house but despite the proximity, she rarely visited. There was little point — her dad no longer knew her. And every time he called her Joanie, her mother's name, it broke her heart just a little bit more.

She'd signed in at the front desk, asked how her dad was doing, got the usual answer: "He's not in any pain. He's happy just watching television and listening to books on CD." That, or a variation of it, was what she heard each time she called or visited.

She was in the armchair opposite her dad, who was in his pajamas and wearing only one slipper but otherwise looked comfortable enough sitting in the love seat in the small living area. His bed was a few feet away and other than a dresser and a bookshelf, the furnishings were sparse.

"Hi, Daddy," Pressley had said when she first arrived, but he waved her quiet and then said, "Shhh, Joanie, that show where people are on an island is on."

She knew it was *Survivor*, his favorite, even before dementia had hijacked him.

Pressley decided to watch the show with him. There would be no talking to him until it was over anyway. Every so often, she looked at her dad. The strong man who'd raised her was gone. Robert James was a shadow of his former self. When she was a child, he seemed to Pressley to be indomitable, tall and broad, a pillar of strength, both physically and emotionally. She'd go to him when she had a problem and he'd fix it. He'd sit her down, ask her what was wrong, take a moment to think, and then come up with three different ways to help. He left the ultimate decision to her, saying the choice should always be hers. But now, without her guiding light, she was lost.

Finally, with *Survivor* over, he turned his attention to her.

"Hi, Joanie!" he said perkily as if suddenly noticing her.

"It me, Dad, Pressley," she replied.

His smile faltered, but only for a second. "Joanie, honey, would you mind pouring me a drink?"

Pressley smiled sadly and didn't move. With the prospect of a drink soon forgotten, he spoke again, "We going to your mother's this weekend? God, I hate going out there. Why don't you go? Take Pressley with you. I just wanna stay home and relax."

Once every month, they'd make the two-hour drive to her grandparents' house and even though Dad protested every time, he always ended up going along.

"Daddy?" Pressley said, knowing she'd be talking more to herself than her dad. "I've met a man who I really like, but I have a problem. A big problem and I wish so much you were able to help me fix it."

He looked at her, nodded and for a second, Pressley let herself hope he really was listening. She continued, "His name's Hayden and I met him at work. I have a new job now, Dad. I work at an animal shelter. But my problem is that there's a dog there, at the shelter, named Jasper and he bit Hayden, so now, they're going to put him down."

His eyes grew wide and his lips thinned to a line. "Put who down where, Joanie?"

"The vet at the shelter wants to ... to kill a dog that I really like. He's not as bad as everyone thinks, and I know that I can give him a good life." She sighed. "But if they do end up killing the dog, I won't be able to go back to work at the shelter, and everything with Hayden is messed up right now." She ran her hands through her hair. "Tell me what to do. I'm so confused."

"Well, the way I see it is: one, you can leave and get another job. Two, go back even if they kill the dog, or three, fight for the dog and fight for the man. The choice is yours. The ultimate decision must be your own."

She couldn't have been more surprised if he'd suddenly started to yodel. "Daddy! Thank you." She wrapped her arms around him and he impatiently patted her on the back with one hand.

"Will you get me my drink now, Joanie?"

~ Seventeen ~

Jasper was curled up comfortably in a ball, but he wasn't in his kennel; instead, he was wrapped in a blanket with his large head on Hayden's knee. The poor dog had been chilled to the bone and it took a while for him to warm up. When Hayden got back to the cottage, he dried off Jasper with his blanket, changed into whatever he could find in the closet — which turned out to be an old, musty-smelling terry cloth robe, replaced his wet bandages with an old towel that he'd ripped up into strips, and then built a fire. Both he and Jasper appreciated the comforting heat. The firewood was bone dry and the fire roared to life as soon as the lit match hit it. He figured the wood was from the pile he'd stacked the last time he and Shaun were there. Thinking about that made him want a drink.

Hayden stared down at Jasper and for the first time, he felt something other than apprehension — he felt love. The dog looked up at him in seeming appreciation for saving his life. Could a dog really feel such things? He petted him, tentatively at first but when Jasper responded by licking his hand, he was soon scratching behind the dog's ears and even kissing the top of his head.

He was amazed at what a little love and attention could do. There was still a long way to go and he didn't know how long it would be until Jasper was considered completely safe, but they had made so much progress already. Why hadn't he started this process sooner? The "old" Hayden probably would have, he reminded himself. The "new" Hayden was too absorbed in his own misery to care. When Shaun died, a huge part of him went with her — the best part of him. But now, as he sat on the sofa with Jasper, he was reminded of what Pressley did for him. She brought him back — she saved him just like he had saved Jasper.

In a little while it would be time to get back to the shelter. Time to show off the new and improved Jasper. He anticipated an argument with Janet and Dr. Graham, but he was up to the challenge.

* * * * *

Once back at Paws and Claws, Hayden tried to coax Jasper into his kennel, but the dog sat down in front of the open door and refused to budge.

"Seriously, dude? You ran away from Pressley to come back here, and now you won't get into your own bed?"

Jasper nosed his hand, forcing Hayden to pet him. Hayden smiled and knelt beside the dog, petting him with both hands. Jasper closed his eyes and enjoyed the attention.

"All right then, how about we sleep over here?" He pointed to a carpeted area. It was not exactly spotless, but it offered a little more padding than the cement floor. Hayden pulled the dog's bed from the kennel onto the carpet and found a couple of old blankets for himself. He checked the time on his phone, which he'd retrieved from the dock before leaving the cottage — it was three in the morning.

Hayden used his knapsack as a pillow. It wasn't the ideal place to bed down for the night, but Jasper seemed happy. The dog laid his head on Hayden's arm as if claiming him as his own. Soon, the dog was asleep. Hayden's eyes were sleep-heavy, and he let them close. He drifted off filled with a sense of accomplishment. He'd done it — he'd helped the unhelpable.

* * * * *

"What the hell?" A male voice pulled Hayden from his slumber. Jasper was on his feet instantly, hackles raised, teeth bared.

Hayden grabbed hold of the dog and pulled him close, wrapping an arm around his barrel chest. He hoped to God the dog wouldn't lunge. His arm was already torn up enough, he didn't need the stitches ripping.

"He's fine, he's fine," Hayden said to Dr. Graham. "Just, please, move back a few feet."

The older man did as he was told. "After what that dog did to you, you've got to be crazy, Hayden," he said in a furious whisper. "What are you doing back here and why is that dog loose?"

Hayden led the dog to his kennel. To Hayden's relief, Jasper went willingly this time. He dusted off the dog fur and the other crud that had clung to his clothes from his night on the floor while Jasper let out a low growl from behind him.

"I've been with him all night, Dr. Graham. In that short time, he's come a long way."

"Do you know how worried we were? I wanted to call the police. Janet wanted to call the Westons—"

"No need for any of that. We're back safe and sound." Hayden smiled nervously.

Dr. Graham shook his head disapprovingly and opened his bag.

"No, Doc. You're not touching this dog. I'd been waiting for morning to call Pressley. I'm absolutely convinced that Jasper won't hurt her. He's good with her and he was good with me."

"I was just going to sedate him. Mind telling me where you took the dog? Janet went to your house and said she'd called you a hundred times."

Hayden thought for a moment. Did he really want to give the doctor the blow-by-blow? "It doesn't matter where Jasper and I were. What matters is I was up half the night with him — training him, getting him to trust me — and what I discovered is that he's a good dog. He doesn't deserve to die."

Dr. Graham's expression darkened. "I'm pretty sure the order will come for me to put him down."

Heat rose in Hayden and he felt it color his face. The man in front of him was supposed to be a champion of animals. Was he so jaded that he no longer cared?

"He's not a bad dog. He's just had a bad life. We all deserve a second chance."

"Seems to me he's had plenty of second chances already," the vet shot back.

"Then a last chance."

Dr. Graham shook his head and his lips thinned to a grim line. "Some animals are lost causes. He's run out of chances." The vet moved toward the cage and put a hand on it. Jasper snarled and jumped, trying to clamp on to whatever he could reach.

"See," Dr. Graham said. "Dog's not ever going to be trustworthy. Best for everyone if he's put down. Move over so I can sedate him until I hear from Janet."

Hayden planted his feet solidly. He wasn't as tall as Dr. Graham, but he was broader and more muscular. "This is not going to happen."

The older man huffed his displeasure. "What do you intend to do?"

"I intend to give this dog a home."

"So now you're taking him home?" The vet laughed.

"Not me. Pressley. Jasper's her dog, legally. I'll make damn sure she sues you if you so much as touch him."

"He attacked you—"

They turned in unison to the sound of the steel door at the end of the hall slamming shut. Hayden smiled when he saw Pressley, though he was less than happy with the scowl on Janet's face.

"What's happening?" Janet asked as they neared.

Pressley's eyes darted from Hayden to the dog and back again. "Where'd you go? I heard you took the dog."

"I was with Jasper all night. I did what I should have done in the first place. I helped him." He looked only at Pressley. "I've made a breakthrough. You can even ask the good doctor here. When he came in, he found me asleep with Jasper curled up right beside me." Hayden turned to Dr. Graham, "Tell them what you saw. Did it look like I was in any danger?"

Hayden continued before Dr. Graham could answer, "Before Shaun died, that's what I did — spent time with the animals, especially the ones like Jasper, and it wasn't until I met you that the desire to make a difference returned. It hurt too much to continue the work I did with Shaun now that she's gone. It was like a knife in my heart."

Her face twisted in confusion. "Then why come to work every day and spend time with the strays? Why put yourself through such torture if, like you said, being here is like a knife in your heart?"

He tried to read her emotions, but her words were matter-of-fact. Somehow that hurt more than if she'd been angry with him. He wanted a temper tantrum, or cutting words, instead she seemed genuinely curious.

He answered honestly. "I do love the animals. I want to help them but that was a bond I shared with Shaun and when she died, it was torture to do it alone. It was a constant reminder of her absence in my life." He sighed, threw Janet and Dr. Graham an annoyed look in an effort to get them to skedaddle, but they stayed put. "I haven't let myself get close to the animals like I did before, but I couldn't *not* be here either. Do you understand?"

Pressley nodded but crossed her arms, closing herself up. Maybe it was all the talk about Shaun that was pushing her away. "I'm messing things up pretty good. Can we talk some more after I get things squared away here?"

"What's left to be done?" Pressley's tone was no longer flat but filled with hope. "You said Jasper's made a breakthrough. That means I can take him now, right?" She moved toward the cage.

Dr. Graham addressed Janet: "Well, you're the boss here. What am I supposed to do?"

Janet handed over a piece of paper to the vet.

"What the hell is that?" Hayden asked.

"Might as well tell them," Janet said, her eyes darting from the vet to Hayden and Pressley and then to the ground. "Sorry," she muttered under her breath.

"See for yourself." Dr. Graham handed the paper to Hayden. Pressley was immediately at his side. They read it together.

It was an order of euthanization, signed by the Westons.

She scowled at Janet. "I can't keep doing this! We both saw Dr. Graham come in here last night. Then you called and told me Jasper was given another reprieve, and now, just when Hayden's said he's made progress with him, now, you're telling me he's going to die!"

Hayden chimed in, "This piece of paper is meaningless. You both know as well as I do that the dog can't be put down because I didn't put in an official complaint. There's nothing on record that states Jasper attacked me."

"You're stitched up, for crying out loud," said Dr. Graham. "You had to go to the hospital. They'll have a record of it."

"Sorry, but all they know is that some stray on the street bit me." Hayden smiled. "Pressley is free to take the dog, if she still wants him, but I've got something else in mind. Something I'd like to talk to Pressley about privately."

Janet looked contrite. "I'm sorry," she said again, looking at Pressley. "Do you know how hard it was when I got that order? I had to tell the Westons about Jasper biting Hayden for legal reasons. You told me about it, Pressley. I had no choice." She put a hand on Pressley's arm.

Pressley pulled away. "I have no recollection of that conversation."

Dr. Graham didn't move, though his eyes followed Janet as she made her way out of the kennels to her office.

"I'm not looking for a fight, Doc, but if you are, you're not gonna win this one," Hayden said.

Dr. Graham nodded toward Jasper. "Hope you both understand what you're fighting for and whether he's worth it." He snapped his bag shut. "Go ahead, take him.

I'll have to report it to the Westons. You know that?"

"That's a chance we're willing to take," Hayden answered for himself and Pressley.

~ Eighteen ~

Jasper was in the back seat of Hayden's truck, keeping a watchful eye on Pressley and Hayden as they sat by the window having coffee at the Riverside Café. The weather was turning. Soon it would be cold instead of chilly as winter descended, but for a day in mid-November, in South Carolina, it was definitely sweater weather: Pressley's favorite.

  The café was decked out with Santas and poinsettias. It made her wonder if she'd be allowed to decorate the office. And if she'd be allowed to bring in a Christmas tree. She caught herself then. Was she quitting or not? Now that Jasper's life had been spared, at least for the moment, she thought perhaps not. She did like the job after all, maybe more than she realized.

She looked at the man sitting across from her. He wore no sweater. It was still T-shirt weather for a man like Hayden. She admired his well-muscled arms and was curious about the tattoo peeking out from under a sleeve. She stopped herself from asking him about it. What if Shaun's name was forever inked in a heart, or worse, her face? That wouldn't be reason enough to be angry with Hayden, but it would still hurt.

He caught her stare and smiled as he lifted his shirt sleeve. "My first love," he said. "Her name was Layla."

Pressley laughed when she saw the tattoo of a bulldog. She touched his arm, caressing the black and white ink, then, looked into his eyes. "You really do love dogs."

"I do. That's why I'm going to take Jasper."

Pressley recoiled, her eyes widening. "But he's *my* dog!"

Hayden leaned forward and spoke softly. "He's still got a ways to go before he can really be anybody's pet. I can't in good conscience let you have him just yet."

"He loves me—"

Hayden stilled her with a hand, and a look that said, please let me finish.

"He's a good dog. Don't get me wrong, but I have to make one hundred percent sure he's not going to hurt you. I'll take him home, then start bringing him to work with me when I think he's ready, so you can see him every day. I should never have let you take him in the first place. I was selfish and stupid. But I still believe in Jasper and, one day, he'll be yours."

Pressley looked over at the dog, who was sniffing the air through the partially open window. Maybe Hayden was right. He was a big, strong dog and she had been worried about whether she'd be able to handle him.

"Okay, that sounds fair." She smiled, and Hayden smiled too.

He moved to the chair beside her and put an arm around her shoulders. "Look at him. I think I'm in for a whole lotta trouble." He laughed.

"Shaun would want this, too," Pressley said.

"No!" He took her hand. "I'm not doing this for Shaun. I'm doing this for you, Pressley. Did I love Shaun? Yes. Do I miss her? Yes. But when I look at old Jasper there messing up the back seat of my brand-new truck, I can't help but believe that in this life, we're given more than one shot at happiness. He's a living example of that. You and I are giving him one last chance! Meeting you may be my last chance, too." He cleared his throat and his expression turned serious. "Pressley, I've fallen for you. It doesn't take a man like me months or years to know what he wants. I knew it the first time I set eyes on you. I want you in my life. You've given me hope again and now I realize my life didn't end when Shaun's did. I'm still here and I deserve to be happy. I hope you feel the same way about me." He kissed her — a sweet soft kiss that sent a jolt right down to her toes. "Will you give me a chance?"

"Absolutely!" she said enthusiastically.

* * * * *

They'd stopped at Pressley's to pick up Jasper's belongings before heading to Hayden's place. Although his house was smaller than hers, his yard was more suited to Jasper — with a tall wooden fence that was much higher than her chain-linked one.

The fact he had good taste surprised her. She hadn't expected the tasteful decorations she was now admiring — the harvest table in the dining room, the comfy-looking brown leather sofas in the family room, with the burnt-orange accents. The modern décor in the kitchen with the round glass and chrome table and dazzling silver light fixture above it. Four white leather chairs were tucked in around it and a large glass container filled with light blue accent pieces sat in the center on a wooden serving tray. Why hadn't she noticed all this the first time she'd been at his house?

She briefly wondered if it was Shaun who'd been responsible for the décor. In the end, she decided it didn't matter. If Hayden was willing to move on, she was too.

"I've got two empty bedrooms. I'll put Jasper's stuff in one of them, but I imagine he might like to sleep with me. I think that would be good for him, actually," Hayden said.

Pressley held the leash as Jasper nosed around, sniffing what he could. He strained on the lead, almost pulling Pressley off her feet. He was a handsome specimen and was all muscle, much like Hayden, she thought with amusement.

"You want me to lead him around the house, so he can check out his new surroundings?" she asked.

"Nah, let him loose. He's not showing signs of anxiety. He'll be okay. He needs to have a little control, so he feels safe." She unclipped the leash, and Jasper trotted away to explore.

Pressley's heart took off in a sprint once the dog was out of sight. "Hayden, shouldn't we watch him? He might, I don't know, ruin something?" She thought of how the dog had peed on her carpet.

"Don't be such a worrywart. I'll be right back — just let me take these things upstairs."

Pressley walked into the kitchen, looking for the dog, but he wasn't there. She tried the family room: no dog. The main floor wasn't large. There weren't many places for him to get to but when she walked down the hallway, she not only saw him but heard him, too. Jasper was sitting at the front door whining.

"Ah, buddy," she said in a high-pitched, friendly voice. "You still think the shelter's your home, don't you?" She scratched his neck, trying to get his attention, but his eyes were trained to the outside world.

Hayden came up behind her. "What's wrong?"

"I have a feeling you're going to have a tough time convincing him this is his home. He's only known the shelter."

"And that horrible place he was taken from before he got to Paws and Claws," Hayden added. "But never mind that." He produced a tennis ball. "Who's up for a game of catch?"

~ Nineteen ~

Monday, May 24th

Pressley finally had to look away from the flash of cameras. Her face hurt from smiling for so long. It was the official opening day of the New Beginnings Animal Shelter she and Hayden started just a month ago. They'd wanted to hold the grand opening on a day that held significance, and today was it. May 24th was Pressley's twenty-eighth birthday.

Two town councilors and the mayor showed up for the ribbon-cutting ceremony along with friends, family, and townsfolk. Pressley's dad was at the front of the crowd along with one of his caretakers from the home.

The ceremony seemed to take forever as the reporters from the local paper covering the event, which was big news in their small town, hollered for Pressley and Hayden to look this way and that. Janet was in the crowd too, waving and smiling. She still ran Paws and Claws but was grateful to have another shelter in town to take on some of the pressure.

Pressley held a pair of oversized scissors, and they were heavy. Finally, with Hayden's help, they cut through the large red ribbon, which ran across the front door of the shelter.

New Beginnings was a no-kill shelter like Paws and Claws, but Pressley and Hayden decided that not a single animal would be put down unless it was absolutely necessary, and that meant sick and nothing else. They had two of the finest animal trainers on staff and would rely on them to rehabilitate the cats and dogs other people saw as lost causes, and even if a forever home couldn't be found, those animals would live out the rest of their days at the shelter.

After the pomp and ceremony, Pressley and Hayden said a few words, gave a quick interview and were relieved to finally be back at work. Just like at Paws and Claws, Pressley worked mainly in the office, but also helped take care of the animals. Hayden did all the maintenance and any heavy lifting that needed to be done. He was indispensable, building storage areas, setting up kennels, assessing the intake animals as well as giving them plenty of attention.

And there were volunteers, mostly teenagers from the community and a few older ladies who stopped by whenever they had time.

Pressley handled the social media and marketing duties, but the thing she loved best — besides running a business that she loved, with the man she loved — was that Jasper was there with them all day. He had the run of the place and would sometimes hang out with Hayden and at other times, curl up in the bed

Pressley had for him beside her desk. He was nothing less than a miracle and a constant reminder that with love, affection, and attention, anything was possible.

He came home with them at the end of the day, too. When Hayden moved in with Pressley, the first thing he did was erect a tall wooden fence around the perimeter of the yard, even though it was doubtful Jasper would ever try to escape again. They'd bought the dog a large memory foam bed and placed it in their bedroom, though he more often than not, jumped up into their bed during the night and snuggled in between them.

Pressley surveyed the office. It was cozy and clean and felt like a home away from home. She took in a breath and let it out slowly. She smiled at how much her life had changed in a matter of months! She'd gone from a woman with no purpose, lost in herself, feeling awkward and alone, to a woman who had everything. She'd finally let down her guard and freed the powerful, confident woman inside her.

Hayden snuck up behind her, wrapped his arms around her waist and kissed her neck. Her hair was a little shorter now, but she wore it down. No more prim and proper buns for Pressley. The scruff of his neatly trimmed beard tickled her cheek. She turned to kiss him.

"Let's go out for a bit," he suggested.

"But we've got work to do."

"And, we're the bosses around here. We can take a break whenever we want. I'll get Charlene to come up to the office. Let's go out for just a while. It's a beautiful day. Come on, we'll take Jasper for a walk." His smile was big and his dimples irresistible.

She reminded herself that she was now the new and improved Pressley, no more fuddy-duddy stick-in-the-mud sensibilities. "Okay," she acquiesced, kissing him again.

Last Chances

* * * * *

Cranbrook Park was peaceful and quiet on that day in May. The occasional jogger bobbed past and a few people inhabited the benches, feeding the pigeons. Pressley had to admit it was wonderful to be out in nature and to feel the warmth of the sun on her face. They'd found a secluded spot with a large grassy area. Hayden threw a ball for Jasper who eagerly played fetch until he was about to collapse. When he'd finally had enough, he drank endlessly from his water bowl and then found a spot to sun himself in.

"You know," Hayden began, "look at us, all of us — you, me, and even Jasper. We're a family." He smiled brightly. "The three of us used to be singular puzzle pieces, all looking for the rest of the pieces, so we could fit together." They were sitting side by side on the grass. Hayden moved over until he was directly in front of Pressley and took her hand in his. "We've accomplished so much in such a short amount of time. Imagine what we'll be able to accomplish in a lifetime." He dug into his pocket and produced a square-cut, yellow diamond ring in a platinum setting. He held it up in front of her between his thumb and pointer finger.

Pressley gasped, a hand flew to her mouth, and her eyes filled with tears.

Hayden continued, "You know, I figured whatever chance at love that came my way after Shaun died would be a distant second to what I had with her, but you've proven that to be untrue. You've shown me that love doesn't end, or just stop when you lose someone special. Life can be a wonder if you open your eyes and your heart enough to recognize the remarkable things that come your way. When I met you, I had a hole in me that I desperately tried to fill. I filled it with anger, I filled it with booze, I filled it with self-pity, and guilt, but when I met you, I realized that maybe, just maybe, I could fill that emptiness with love again. You and Jasper gave me back my life, and I want to spend the rest of it with you." He levered himself up to a knee and poised the ring in front of her finger. "Will you do me the honor of being my wife?"

"Yes!" Pressley practically yelled and when Hayden slid the ring onto her finger, she was instantly in his arms, kissing him. Jasper bounded over barking and jumping playfully, wanting to get in on the action.

Pressley and Hayden parted enough for Jasper to wriggle his way in between them. He doled out slobbery kisses and barked excitedly as if to proclaim that last chances were the sweetest of them all.

~ About the Author ~

Jeanne Bannon is a USA Today bestselling author. She has worked in the publishing industry for over twenty-five years, first as a freelance journalist, then as an in-house editor for LexisNexis. She currently works as a freelance editor and writer.

When not reading or writing, Jeanne enjoys spending time with her daughters, Nina and Sara and her husband, David. She's also the proud mother of two fur babies, a cuddly and affectionate Boston Terrier named Lila and Spencer, a rambunctious tabby, who can be a very bad boy.

~ Discover more about Jeanne Bannon ~

Visit http://www.jeannebannon.com or sign up to receive her [exclusive reader newsletter](#).

You can also find her on [Twitter](#) and [Facebook](#).

~ Other Books by Jeanne Bannon ~

Invisible

Nowhere to Run

Lost and Found

Love Bites

Beautiful Monster – The Exchange (book one)

Beautiful Monster – The Hunt (book two)

Proof

Made in the USA
Columbia, SC
03 February 2018